Drag Me Down

A Rockstar Romance Series

Abigail Glenn

Portal World Publishing

Author's Note

Drag Me Down spans a few countries and many U.S. cities. While some venues, monuments, restaurants, hotels, etc. are real places I've visited, they may have been modified to fit this story. Also, one of my characters is British, so words have been tailored accordingly as much as I was able to catch with my American eye. Apologies to the British for possibly butchering things!

In other words, I don't always know what the hell I'm talking about, but I've done my best to research and portray things as realistically as possible. Please take this book for what it is: a spicy, emotional journey of two wounded musicians who fall in love.

Hope you enjoy!

Contents

Trigger Warnings

Depression, suicide, substance abuse
Mention of self-harm and physical abuse

Playlist

Nazareth – Sleep Token
To the Hellfire – Lorna Shore
Schism – Tool
Sleeping on the Blacktop – Colter Wall
Nocturnes, Op. 9: No. 2, Andante in E-flat major – Frédéric Chopin, Finghin Collins
Risk – FKJ, Bas
Pisces – Jinjer
Adagio for Strings, Op. 11 – Samuel Barber, David Parry, London Philharmonic Orchestra
Mouth of Kala – Gojira
Straight Lines – Vola
Blood Sport – Sleep Token
Sugar – Sleep Token
Sober – Tool
Descent – Orbit Culture
Are You Really Okay? – Sleep Token
ABC (feat. Sophia Black) – Polyphia, Sophia Black

Atonement Tour Schedule

London, UK
Derby, UK
Paris, France
New York City, NY
Boston, MA
Atlanta, GA
Nashville, TN
Charleston, VA
Indianapolis, IN
Louisville, KY
Columbus, OH
Detroit, MI
Chicago, IL
Madison, WI
Des Moines, IA
Kansas City, MO
Denver, CO
Colorado Springs, CO
Albuquerque, NM
Austin, TX
Dallas, TX
Houston, TX
Little Rock, AR
Oklahoma City, OK
Phoenix, AZ
Salt Lake City, UT
Boise, ID
Las Vegas, NV

Los Angeles, CA
Sacramento, CA
Portland, OR
Seattle, WA
Vancouver, CA

ONE
Z

I don't know what the fuck I'm doing here.

The thought rattles around in my chaotic brain as spotlights burn my retinas, blinding me to the inhabitants of the grungy underground bar. Tucking my chin, I hide behind the unruly locks of my ink black hair and dissolve into muscle memory, letting it guide my long, nimble fingers over the fret of my acoustic guitar.

It's been too long since I've allowed my throat to produce anything that resembles sound other than heathen grunts and mumbled speech, and my lack of practice performing is audible in the quiver of the notes I force through my lips.

The crowd doesn't care one way or another if I'm any good. It's a proper bribery situation. They came for Selma's famous cocktails, only to be submitted to my awkward thirty-minute performance to test out the same songs I've been stuck on writing for months now. Should they pass my own critical judgment, I'll finally post them up for licensing.

God knows I need the royalties.

People continue their drunken, sloppy conversations while I tear my soul apart on the small stage. In a smoky, low-lit room of nobodies, I am nobody, too. I can almost disappear.

Guilt winds barbed vines around my heart. I shouldn't be here, no matter the shit state of my finances. It's a dishonour to his memory.

But what else am I supposed to do? I've poured everything into music. I'm in no right mind to find a job outside of selling songs. And even if I were well off, I still wouldn't be able to cut music out of my life. Without it, I wouldn't have a purpose.

Shoving all of that mottled, gnarled emotion into my last song, I drown in the low, haunting tone my vocal cords finally produce. I hold out notes, chasing that hit of dopamine from somewhere in the pit I've found myself dwelling in.

When I'm finished, I crack my eyes open and blink a few times. Selma hits the switch to turn the spotlights off, knowing I prefer to slink off stage without conversation. It's been a few months since I've played a set here, but I've come to form somewhat of a friendship with her over the years, despite my aversion to London.

The return of my surroundings is harsh and jarring, like stepping out into the midday sun when I've spent years in the dark or jumping from a hot tub into a cold pool.

Slowly, my brain registers that I'm not on tour. There aren't thousands of fans shouting back at me. I'm in a cramped, dark bar sunk into London, and there are only a couple dozen heads positioned around pub tables, all turned away from me.

A few pity claps sound out as I release a shaky breath and rise from my stool. Initiate shutdown mode. Facing my fears never gets easier. I stare them down constantly, and all this exercise serves to do is shave away at my insides until I'm a raw husk. On the rare occasion that I do step on stage, I waste days after in fallout from a reality that is already hellish enough.

Part of me knows it's possible to climb out of my self-made pit, but I'm staring up at the opening from thirty feet down with nothing but my hands and feet to get me out and the broken pieces of me whispering in my ear that I don't deserve to escape.

Suddenly, I'm struck with the urge to turn around and give the crowd one more glance, almost as if a magnetic pull has a hold of me. My gaze locks on a pair of whiskey eyes. Gripping the fret of my guitar tighter, I take in his strong form lounged at the bar. He's got a shag of blonde hair that hangs down one side of his head, the sides shaved tight to his scalp. Dressed in a sleeveless white t-shirt with the sides cut down to his waist, his tanned, inked skin is on display like artwork. And when he reaches for his pint, I glimpse the shine of a bar through his nipple.

As I'm mapping him out, his fiery gaze slowly drags from my combat boots, to my ripped black jeans that hug slim calves and thighs, to my paint-splattered band shirt under a plaid button-up, and then lands back on my eyes.

Heat licks up the back of my neck, scorching my ears and cheeks as blood rushes low in my gut. I swallow, watching him raise his pint and take a long swig from it. Condensation rolls down the glass to kiss his veiny hand. The bob of his Adam's apple shouldn't have me worked up, but somehow I can't shake the desire to cross the bar and run my tongue over it.

He's incredibly sexy.

My entire body tenses at that thought. Not that I haven't come to terms with my sexuality. That ship sailed fifteen years ago. It's just, I haven't felt that flicker of... well, anything positive, in a long time.

Suffocating the excited things fluttering in my hollow chest, I quickly slink off stage and pack up my guitar in its case. Head lowered, I stride for the exit, mentally preparing for another late night in my rental house where I will continuously bang my forehead against my desk, littered with half-finished songs I plan to sell to artists with the actual fortitude to stand up on a real stage. No hood or mask to hide behind. No fake name to keep their real life private from the media.

"Z!" A high-pitched voice rings out above the chatter.

Cringing internally, I slow my pace and turn toward Selma, the owner of the bar, her bubblegum pink bob of hair a shock of colour in the dim space. She's helped keep me fed and clothed by allowing me to perform here whenever I find my nerve. Though we both know the locals are growing tired with my set. It's far too sappy for this scene. It's only a matter of time before Selma's sympathy dries up and I'll be out of another stream of income.

"Great performance tonight." She gives me a wink with her long fake lashes. "Are we going to get anything new? How about Friday night?"

I sink my teeth into my bottom lip as my eyes flit to the enchanting bloke across the bar. Heat floods my system when I find him still staring at me with those detrimental eyes, their depths warm like honey, viscous enough to trap me.

As if he hasn't already thrown me for a loop, a slow smile eases onto his handsome face.

"I'm... uh... working on something," I reply, giving in to the nervous tick of running my hand along the back of my sweaty neck.

When the guy shifts his focus to the man sitting next to him—a perplexing contradiction of soft features, long black waves of hair, corded muscle, and more ink than visible skin—my curiosity runs wild, starting at tattoo artists and quickly ending at musicians when I glimpse the guitar pick dancing between the second guy's long fingers.

Panic grips me around the throat. Though the likelihood of them recognising me is slim. *No reason to spiral out.*

Selma catches me checking them out and waggles her brows. "Guests from across the pond." She leans over to hand me the tips she always collects for me. "Told me to keep it hush-hush, but you're a musician, too, and I know you won't run your mouth. Ever heard of the band Atonement?"

My brows furrow. I give a little shake of my head as I tuck the measly bills into my tight pocket. I've purposely kept my blinders up when it comes to the music scene, my previous bandmate's threat still branded into my brain.

"Might want to have a look tonight. You just performed for metal gods, love."

Dropping back behind the counter, she flashes me a coy smile and gives me a little wave with vampire-sharp nails before returning to the tending bar. "Catch you Friday, Z."

Lingering nerves from my performance kick up another mosh pit in my chest. I don't dare another glance at the two beautiful guys across the bar.

Had I any fucking courage in my body, I'd stick around long enough to reject another performance so soon. Two days doesn't leave me enough time to recover from this one.

Instead, I turn and run from the bar.

I t's just the kind of place Liam, the lead guitarist for Atonement, wouldn't frequent. Which is exactly why I drag him down the tight staircase into the hidden bar, lured by the soulful melody resounding behind the peeling, red-painted door.

We've toured Europe before, and while London isn't one of my favorite cities to visit, I still find a thrill in exploring local joints and offending the British with my ADHD American energy.

Honestly, all the overseas cities we've performed at have been a blast. The food here tastes so much better. Okay, Iceland: what the hell kind of crack do you put in your pancakes?

The locals have been welcoming for the most part, too. Though, that might have something to do with our celebrity status. Or the amount of money I've dropped on said crack pancakes.

Metal gods, we've been titled in the latest magazines and online articles. The freshest aggressive band to hit the festival circuit, even though we've been around for eight years. Eight tireless fucking years. That's not counting the years prior with other bands, fighting to claw my way into the spotlight. Most of my twenties were spent on the road, in a plane, on a stage, or in a hotel room, and not all of them high-class.

I crack a toothy grin at the sketch interior of the bar. Windowless, bathed in old cigarette stench, and teeming with moody, grunge vibes from the dark paint to the choice abstract artwork. It reminds me of some of the first venues we played as a band.

Immediately to our left, there's a U-shaped bar. Two tattooed women flit behind it like dragonflies locked in an orchestrated dance, serving up neon cocktails decked out with chunks of fruit. Dozens of high-top tables are scattered around the room, half of which are occupied.

And in the back of the rectangular space, there's a tiny stage where a young guy is hunched over his acoustic guitar, strumming out a tune that reaches inside me and grips me at my core.

His head lifts to the microphone, and I catch a glimpse of the face hidden beneath long, black locks of hair. My jaw actually drops. His features are so soft, his lips full and eyes a pure, glacier blue. His skin is flawless, like porcelain. One wrong hit, and I think he might shatter.

I fall into his lyrics instantly.

A river of blood is all I see

As the current claims me, enslaving me to its chaotic ways

I'm forever swimming, swimming upstream

Prayers for drought rip free as cursed screams

But the fear of what I'll see when that river runs dry

What else will I find, beyond the cleaned bones of the forgotten?

The phantoms of last breaths, last sighs, last whispers, last cries?

Liam presses in against my shoulder to yell in my ear. "He's good."

I can only nod, too drawn in to elaborate on all the ways this man has a death grip on my senses right now.

Fumbling for a stool at the bar, I drop onto it and continue my examination. I'm not sure if he's being purposeful with his quick vibrato or if he's just nervous. The chords he plays are unique and well-practiced. But his stage presence? Absolute garbage. Zero eye contact with the crowd, and no words shared with us between songs.

And yet, I'm in rapture. There's no need for speech beyond this emotional connection. He already has me perched on the edge of my seat, aching to inch myself closer. Closer to that gaping wound in his chest where words flow free, pain reveals itself, and heartache bears its vicious fangs, ready to spread infection.

This right here is what I'm missing.

While some fans swear I made a deal with the devil to acquire my harsh vocals, I've never been complimented for my lyricism or creativity. It shouldn't bother me. Atonement has had tremendous success, something few bands actually achieve.

The other guys in the band don't care so much what I scream into the mic on stage, as long as we keep climbing the ladder of success. As long as I continue to pummel our fans into the ground with my intensity.

But that wounded little kid in me that's still seeking approval wants more. He tells me fame alone won't be enough to prove to my family that I chose the right path in not pursuing a secondary education and standard career.

I want more than that. I want to explore genres. Blend them together in new ways. I want to produce quality that is worthy of the fame we've achieved. That's how we keep the fans around long term. I don't want to keep pushing out generic metal. How many times can we *watch the world burn* for god's sake?

The answer's once, okay?

That little prickle of want has my mouth opening and closing as I weigh the decision of taking on an additional project. Of approaching this guy for some sort of collaboration, whatever that may look like.

My focus *should* be entirely on Atonement, as it has been for years.

A woman with a pink bob hops over to us. "You boys need something to drink?"

Liam flashes his signature, slow-burn grin, the one that wins every time, and leans over the counter. I roll my eyes but can't help my own smart little smirk.

Always on the hunt for the next woman to warm his sheets. It's why I demand a separate bedroom while on tour. It's harder to tune out Liam's sexual activities on the tour bus, though. He has the appetite that could rival the caloric intake of a bodybuilder or professional sports player.

Which is funny because he's practically built like one. He spends enough time working out to be one.

She slaps a palm on the counter. "Don't even try it, pretty boy. I'm too old for you."

"Oh, I like her. She doesn't hold back punches." I chuckle.

"What's your name?" Liam asks, the wattage on his smile creeping higher as he drops onto a stool beside me.

She pops her gum. "Selma. I own the place."

"Nice to meet you, Selma." Liam tosses a crisp twenty-pound note next to her petite hand. "Strong stuff for me–a bottle of Coke, please."

"Coke and rum?" She cocks a brow.

"Minus the rum. I don't drink."

She moves her hand to her hip, leaning into it. "You came into my bar and you don't drink?"

Liam jabs his thumb at me. "He kidnapped me and dragged me here. Call for help."

His tone is so dry the bartender's wide eyes actually slide to me, sizing me up. Then her mouth falls open, forming the perfect o-shape.

"Ah, shit," I mutter, dropping my forehead into a palm. Here I thought we wouldn't be recognized in a low-key joint. My face must convey the need to maintain discretion because Selma quickly fixes her expression and gives me a little wink.

"Your secret's safe with me, *Mykhail*."

I beam back at her, my heart finding its normal rhythm again. "Selma, I might never leave your place. I'll have a beer. Your choice."

"Long as you keep paying, I'll house you forever, love." She winks again, then snatches up the collection of bills Liam and I piled up for her.

Thank you sweet baby Jesus, she's letting it drop that she knows who I am. I make a mental note to give Liam shit later for not being recognized. Usually, he's the first to be called out in public. He's got that bad boy rockstar aura surrounding him. Might be all the abstract and geometric tattoos—angels and demons crossing paths—and the envious waves of long, dark hair. Or the gothic rings. I've never understood the fascination with rings.

Tucking a few more pounds into both tip jars, one for the bartenders and the other for the performer, I settle back into my detailed analysis of the exquisite specimen on stage. Definitely in full control of his voice. He's so intentional with his musicality, it's... mesmerizing.

I lean my shoulder against Liam's solid form. "Classically trained?"

Liam gives a nod. "For sure."

Chewing on my lip, I can't help but ask, "Think we could corner him and threaten him into writing us something?"

Liam sucks down half his Coke, leaving me hanging with a quickening pulse as I wait for his reaction. "Not sure that's how it works."

Frowning, I straighten up on my seat. I get that Malek and Griff want to stay firmly planted in their metal roots, but I'm a no labels kind of guy, and constantly channeling my inner demons on stage is starting to wear me out at thirty-one years of age. Not that I'd admit that to the guys when we're at the peak of success.

But I'd love to try out something slower, with more of an edged impact, like this guy on stage. And that has absolutely nothing to do with the looming expiration date on Liam's participation in Atonement. Nope. None at all.

Selma wanders back over with a pint of dark beer and slides it across the table. Wrapping a hand around the cold glass, I suck down a long gulp, then tip my head to the stage as she waits for my approval on the beer. "Who's the musician?"

"Local guy. Plays here every now and then to make a few pounds. I told him he ought to send a sample to a record label or something. His talent is wasted here."

"It sure fucking is," I murmur, eyes sliding to the stage again. When I realize how my words might be taken, my head snaps back to Selma. "Not that your bar sucks or anything—"

She waves a hand at me. "I get it, rockstar. Don't shit your pants."

For good measure, I drop a handful of coins into the tip jar. Somehow, my pockets are always overflowing with them when we tour overseas. Selma gives me a brilliant smile.

The musician's final song rips my throbbing heart out of its cage and stomps on it, touching on what I interpret to be a story about witnessing the death of a loved one.

This is my undefeated test
Why won't you take your wings so we can both rest?
And if you never learned how to fly
If you fail to reach those sunlight clouds
I promise to carry you up the sky
Leave all your mortal burdens behind
As I deliver you home for good

He ends on a lingering low note, his head bowed. The urge to move to him and ask if he's okay nearly has me off my stool. Spotlights over the stage click off, and after a few staggered claps, he seems to come back down to this plane of existence from heaven.

When he stands, tall and lean, his gaze sweeps out, meeting mine from across the bar. My heart pounds all the way up in my throat. I'm not really sure why I do it, but I let my eyes peruse up his body, knowing he's fully aware.

Needing something to chill the inferno burning in my chest, I take a long draw from my beer. Why is my pulse hammering like I just ran from a surprise mountain lion on a hike through the woods? This is what a true artist does, right? Manipulates the crowd like a master of puppets. Twists their insides, hellbent on leaving them in pieces when the show is over. Leaving them with something to talk about.

Fuck, I want... What do I want? To join in his summonings of pain? To accompany him on a journey through hell and back so I can find wings, too?

My fingers twitch, aching to run along the fret of a guitar. I had this same feeling when we witnessed Griff and Malek playing at some grungy Austin venue years ago, right before we formed Atonement and rose to the top.

This guy could be at the top.

I shouldn't want in on that. I shouldn't be thinking about anything outside of Atonement. It's selfish, especially knowing we're going to lose Liam to the next stage of his life. The old man thinks he's ready to settle down and buy a recording studio somewhere in Dallas, along with a permanent residence. I can't leave Griff and Malek hanging.

Swiftly, the guy moves off stage. I play it cool, though wild energy is practically vibrating beneath my skin. Lingering at the bar, I'm confident he'll check in with Selma to collect tips before he heads out. Maybe he'll sit down for a drink or two and we can chat.

I keep eyes on him as he cuts through the tables with his guitar in tow. Jesus, he's even taller off stage, rising well above the patrons on high stools. Do I look smaller when I'm on stage? I mean, I'm not built like a freight train—that's Liam—but I do have definition from a bit of light gym time with Liam and hours of high-energy performing.

Panic grips me when he doesn't stop at the bar. *Shit, he's going to bail.* My hands grip the counter as I rise, prepared to give chase. The gnawing hunger to understand the formula of the power he's crafted needs to be tamed.

When my interest is peaked, I go after something whole-heartedly. Picked up my first guitar in fourth grade. I won the school talent show that same year. Offered up cigarettes and jokes for hours when I first ran into Griff and Malek blasting beats at that venue. We were best buds and bandmates before the night was over. Quit high school senior year to focus on music. Released our first album the next summer and played a sold out show soon after before landing an opening gig for a larger band on tour.

And when my last relationship bombed years ago, after discovering my girl with another dude's dick shoved halfway down her throat, I threw everything into Atonement. Every aspect of my life, sunrise to bleeding sunset.

Thankfully, Selma calls the musician over to the bar. "Z!"

Z? Is that a nickname? What could that be short for? Zach? Zade? Why do I care? Oh, hey obsessive part of my brain! Can we not? I only care because of his music. But if I knew his name, I could look him up online. Possibly find his social media or a Spotify account. Has he released any songs?

He gives me another look as he reaches the bar, and I break into a genuine smile. His eyes are ice chips that somehow awaken wildfire in my veins. His features are so beautifully put together. He can't be fucking real.

My hand grips my cold pint tighter. Am I...attracted to him? Is that what's happening right now? Because that's brand spanking new. Or is it truly his talent that has me practically drooling to speak with him?

Turning to Liam, prickles of nerves and buzzing excitement fight for attention in my chest. "I'm going to approach him."

"Hail." Liam's tone is cautious, recognizing that reckless streak in me to chase after *more*. Always eager to fill that void inside of me. The desire for approval. For fame. For...fucking something I don't even know I'm missing.

A quick spurt of anger flickers in my gut. I extinguish it when I remind myself that I haven't been open with Liam about my recent thoughts. The restlessness in my bones that I haven't yet achieved my potential. That I haven't found my place in the music world just yet, despite the sheer amount of time and effort I've put in.

Hell, I haven't told anyone in Atonement that my brain has been wandering down other possible paths...

I lick my lips and pivot my body fully to Liam, needing him to understand. Humor comes easy to me. So easy, most people don't know when to take me seriously. "For a side project, maybe. Or to help me write new material for Atonement. I know we just dropped an awesome album, but fans are going to want greater things from us moving forward. And when you're no longer around because you're a boss producer, I'll be left to figure out how to do that. How to keep elevating Malek and Griff."

What I really want to say is, *how do I carry on without you?* Since we started up the band, we've been together almost nonstop.

Liam stares back at me with his steady, dark brown eyes. They're almost eerily black in the dim bar. We've been friends since the fourth grade, so he knows better than anyone else how hard I latch onto things I want. How proactive I can be, especially when something dreadful is chomping at my heels, like his inevitable abandonment of the thing that started with us at the core.

He cocks a dark brow. "A side project."

Another band? is the real question he's asking. *What would Griff and Malek think? Both of us ditching out on them?*

"Look at Maynard! He has like three bands and still manages to juggle everything."

"Be honest, Hail. You can't juggle worth shit," Liam counters, folding his arms over his chest.

My heart constricts. "You know Atonement has always been my number one priority. Wait, why am I even asking you for permission?"

Liam chuckles. "Because you're trying to convince yourself that you're making a good decision." Downing his Coke, he sighs and runs his tattooed hand down his sharp jawline. "Look, I'm sure my lawyer can draft up whatever you decide you need from this guy, if he's even interested. Just know, Sondra's going to have questions, and so are Malek and Griff. Shit, I have questions."

"Okay, yeah. I get that." I nod fervently, not even certain myself what I need out of this or how to explain it to our band manager. My heart lurches as I whip back around to lock eyes with Z along the bar.

Only, the angel I planned to leash is gone.

Three

Z

P er routine, I start banging my head against my desk around one in the morning. Between too many cups of black coffee and scribbling out endless pages of shit lyrics, this self-inflicted pain continues until sunrise.

Dragging my body upright into a somewhat human form, I stand on weary legs and shuffle into the outdated galley kitchen to make a third pot of coffee. Then I pop a Prozac and swish it down with the cold dredges left in my mug.

I've been on this new antidepressant for a day now, and it's only served to take me through a whirlwind of emotions in the span of twelve hours. Slurred words like a state of inebriation to start, so much so that I worried about my performance at Selma's bar last night. But as soon as I stepped out of the cab, my brain chemicals decided to even out enough for me to make it through all of my songs without crippling anxiety.

And then I spent the evening down, riding waves of lows unlike anything I've experienced. Several times, I ended up on the bathroom tiles, Googling side effects, worried something might actually be severely wrong with me, and then frustrated with myself for actually caring about the state of my health.

Should I stick this medication out or drop it like I've done with so many others? How many more trips on the pharmacy merry-go-round am I going to pay for? Is my brain doomed to be permanently fucked?

Regardless of what my brain *needs*, it doesn't seem to want help. I suppose I should call my psychiatrist about it, but I'm not really feeling up to a conversation with her when she literally doesn't give a shit about me and just wants to push pills.

Running my hands through my hair, I decide on a shower. I didn't even get to that last night. Just remained in my sweaty, filthy street clothes and bled agony onto paper until my vision blurred and my hands shook from overdosing caffeine in substitution of what I really craved. Something to put me out of my misery for a little while. I'm not convinced that itch will ever leave me, almost like it's coded into my very DNA.

After methodically cleaning myself, I dress in black cargo trousers and a dark, form-fitted t-shirt. With my hands braced on the sink, I lift my head to the mirror and stare back at the reflection I try to avoid most days.

All I see is *his* face. Instantly, I'm sick to my stomach. My spine curls forward as the room tilts sideways. One deep breath in and then I'm spilling my guts, purging the medicine I just took in union with bitter coffee.

When I'm sure my stomach is empty, I peel off my clothes and shower all over again because I don't know what to do with myself, and I can't get rid of the acidic taste in my mouth or the hollow ache in my chest.

I'm a waste of skin and bones and nerves that only malfunction.

Redressed, I shuffle back into the small living room and plop onto the firm Ikea couch that still smells like the packaging. All of a month and a half in this tiny, archaic rental house, and I've still only furnished it with the essentials. It's the most roots I've put down in five years. I can't bring myself to hang anything on the walls, quite certain a single nail would cause them to crumple like tissue paper.

Flipping open my laptop, my fingers hover over the keys for a few breaths. I sink my teeth into my bottom lip and type in Atonement.

Not surprising. The lead vocalist, Mykhail "Hail" Koval, is just as photogenic as he was breathtaking in person. His wide smile radiates warmth, and his rich, light brown eyes spark with vitality.

Honestly, all of them are easy on the eyes. Liam, their lead guitarist, captivates attention much like a black hole, dark and dangerous. Their bassist, Malek, has almost elvish features, blood-red hair, and a wicked cunning grin. And their drummer, Griff, softens their strong angles and eclectic attire with kind eyes and loungewear in most of their photos.

There's a flicker of concern in my brain when I'm disappointed by the lack of details on Hail's personal life. I click on one of their live videos at a festival in Germany, and I'm overwhelmed by the shift in his personality when he takes centre stage. All smiles until the second his hand touches the mic.

He gives the massive crowd no time at all to brace for the wall of sound he barrages them with, summoning guttural screams. His lows draw my pounding heart down into the pit of my stomach. And his highs? They shoot me right back up with a dose of adrenaline, jolting my heart into an erratic rhythm.

The urge to see them live, to experience this up close, grips me with iron strength. Can he stir up this same reaction when I'm standing before him? It's been so long since I've felt a rush like this, a low thrum of something exciting growing deep in my bones.

Five years is a hell of a long time to lurk in the shadows all alone, especially now that I've glimpsed the pillar of light that is Hail. I'm at war with myself over whether or not to chase this.

Without realising it, I've searched their tour dates. They must have a show close by if they're hanging out in London. I'm not surprised to find them booked up at The Dome Thursday night.

My heart gives an extra beat when I see that they're playing at the Download Festival Friday afternoon. Somehow the mouse finds the purchase tickets button. It's an awful lot to spend on one ticket, and I'm not even interested in seeing anyone else perform. I'm so far out of tune with the music world, I don't recognise much of the line-up. If I did, I would most definitely be able to talk myself out of going.

But the tips from last night were more than I expected, and the way Hail was looking at me? The way his voice reaches inside of me to throttle me back to life? I could become addicted to this.

Mentally, I tally how much money I have left for food and bills. Royalties are always slow to trickle in, and my savings is just about wiped clean. What would the media think about that? *Washed up rockstar blows through his fortune and spends his nights tracing grout lines in a run-down bathroom alone.*

Before I can find logic, my heart gives another vigorous thud as my finger clicks the purchase button.

I'm drowning in a sea of heaving, shrieking fans.

To say it's not an all-consuming rush would be a lie. Surrounded by thousands of bodies pouring out excitement, it's impossible not to get a contact high.

The demonic sounds ripping free from Hail's throat skewer me in place. Bolt me onto my little patch of trampled grass near the front of the festival stage. People thrash all around me, but I remain still, feeling untethered from my body. Ascended, as I stare up at a music god, proper flames erupting all around him.

I know I don't know him. One night locking eyes across a grungy bar doesn't even make us acquaintances. But from my continued research each night leading up to their show, I learned that Atonement has blown up in almost every major country after their newly released album of absolute bangers. Hell, I've had their album on repeat for the past two days.

Hail shouldn't mean anything to me. Not when I've only heard his voice through my wireless headphones while staring up at the ceiling in my bedroom for countless hours.

And yet, here I am, being transported by the rage he's channelling as if he's standing a breath away, his fingers reaching out to burrow into my soul like some sort of grim reaper.

At this moment, I can temporarily forget my past. I can dream about the future in music I might have had, before everything fell apart in the span of one nightmarish evening.

Hail curls over the edge of the stage, bringing his head closer to the writhing fans with multicoloured hair, unique piercings, and more ink visible than skin. Their hands outstretch, clawing at the air. Frantic to touch him and break off a piece of him.

It used to bother me how much humans could obsess over someone they don't know.

But here I am.

His eyes find mine, and a flicker of surprise runs through their amber depths as his brows lift slightly. My foolish heart sputters against my ribs, like a frantic bird trapped in a cage. He doesn't break our locked gazes as he pushes out screams, tapping into wounds I don't understand.

We all hurt in different ways, don't we?

The song ends abruptly, but Hail's attention doesn't shift from me. Fans gasp and security flocks as he leaps from the stage. Easing past the bulky, hired help, he effortlessly hoists his body over the metal barrier between the stage and the fans.

Fucking hell. What does he think he's doing? People are going to eat him alive.

Blood pressure rising, I turn and push through the crowd, my shattered heart chugging out a heady warning of self-preservation. Maybe he's not coming for me. Maybe I'm giving too much weight to my existence.

But when I glance behind me, he calls out, as hands grab at his sweaty skin and people scream into his ears.

Why did I think coming here was a good idea? Thank god the fans help to slow his chase, and I make it to the back of the field where people are more dispersed, sprawled out on blankets or slouched in foldable chairs.

Hesitating, I glance around for some place to lose him.

"Hey, dude," he calls again. Calloused fingers brush my arm. How the hell did he catch up to me so fast? "You're the guy from the bar the other night, right?"

Swallowing, I crack my knuckles and regretfully spin around to face him, heart slamming against my ribcage. "Uh... yeah, that's me."

His eyes glimmer with amusement as his smile grows. Picking up on my nervous movements, he takes a step back to give me space. "I knew it! What are you doing here? Are you performing?"

What *could* I say? *No, I'm not in a place to ever perform on a stage like this again? I saw you staring at me two nights ago and couldn't get you out of my head? Did I imagine you checking me out, or am I just overly desperate for any kind of attention? Selma told me you're talented, and I cared enough to check you out for myself? I spent three hours of my morning watching videos of you spitting out water on stage and glistening with sweat like some sort of creep?*

That's why I'm here, right? Because I couldn't drink my fill of him from behind a computer screen in my rundown house. Because I'm a fucking masochist. A loser that desired more of him, but only from the safety of the shadows where I could observe and not engage him.

My eyes dart around to the people watching us. They hover closer, Sharpies and band t-shirts in hand, mouths practically foaming in excitement. Other people pull out their phones to snap pictures. I wince, drawing back from him, but he matches my step and wraps a hand around my wrist. His brows furrow in concern as he gives me a light squeeze.

Oh god, can he feel my pulse practically jumping out of my clammy skin?

"You okay?" he asks gently.

I nod, though the direct attention is messing with my ability to string together words.

His head tilts. "What's your name?"

"Z," I bark out.

"Z." He seems to roll this over in his mind, and then another smile lights up his face. "Z, I'm glad you're here. I actually wanted to talk to you at the bar. Come hang with me for a while, yeah?"

Physically unable to shake my head, though my brain is screaming to abort mission, I let him guide me along the edge of the crowd toward a restricted area where the tour buses are parked. My heartbeat pounds beneath his touch, my eyes focused on his hand softly gripping me.

Wild thoughts run rampant in my head as I pick through my morning research. Could he be...? *No.* There's no way. Nothing online mentioned anything about Mykhail Koval playing for the other team. Honestly, there wasn't much tied to his name beyond his recent success with Atonement and his Texas roots.

Then again, what did the media get right?

I clench my teeth, shoving aside an onslaught of painful memories. Now is *not* the time to spiral down into that darkness.

Even if Hail was interested in men, he would never be interested in me.

He pulls me onto a giant, metallic tour bus. Thankfully, it's void of life, though I glimpsed his band lurking at the back of the stage with the crew.

"Shouldn't you be over there?" I ask, nervously picking at the frayed stitching along my trouser pockets.

He ignores my question, waving a hand at the small kitchen. "Grab a drink. I'm just gonna rinse off real quick."

Then he vanishes into the back, and I'm left standing in the middle of Atonement's tour bus. What if the rest of the band comes back before Hail returns? What if security assumes I'm some rabid fan trying to snap a dick pic of the metal god?

My body temperature spikes. *Get it out of your head, Z.*

I pinch the bridge of my nose for a few deep breaths. Snatching a Coke from the small fridge, I perch on the couch and try to look like I belong here, not like I'm calculating the time it will take me to get arrested. I don't think I'd do well behind bars. I've been called too pretty for a guy, and while I'm quite tall, I'm too lean to hold my own in a proper fight.

A few minutes pass, and Hail strides into view clad in tight black trousers. He's still in the process of tugging on a clean shirt, flashing me a defined, tan stomach. Swirls of beautiful ink cover one side of his body.

Fucking hell. Both nipples pierced. Why do I find that attractive all of a sudden? Maybe because they're attached to this sexy metalhead that somehow exudes warmth like the sun, dimples and all.

I'm struck with curiosity over whether those piercings enhance pleasure. Would he moan and arch his back if I sucked on them? Beg for me to touch him? Tease him? Sink into him?

Hot blood hits my cock, and I jerk my gaze up to meet his eyes as he gives me a crooked smile. "Let's blow this popsicle stand."

"Um, what?" I blink back at him, fingernails pinching away at the loose strings around my sleeves.

Chuckling, he snatches a set of keys from a hook on the small fridge and tilts his head. "Follow me."

He sets a brisk pace across the parking lot. I nearly trip rushing after him. He gives a wave to his bandmates, and I pick out Liam from the night at the bar and my trip down the internet wormhole. Liam tips his chin up in greeting. I manage an awkward hand lift back at him, flushing with heat as the others turn to examine me while I struggle to catch up to Hail.

The headlights of a parked Audi blink ahead of us, and I look between Hail's keys and the black car.

"Wait, we're not actually leaving, are we?"

"That a problem?"

I stop in my tracks, thoroughly confused by the company I've acquired. He lifts a brow at me, then moves to open the passenger door. "You gonna stand there and gape at me forever? Cause I'm kind of in a hurry to get you all to myself."

O *kay, what was that comment?*

Molten eyes rove over me, rich like caramel in the sunlight. Am I reading too much into this, or could Hail Koval be checking me out right now over the top of his rental car? Did I not sleep enough? I *know* for a fact I didn't sleep well. Is this a hallucination? A hostile takeover of my depraved imagination?

Part of my struggle is that I overthink in these types of situations. Is he just being nice? Is this my brain projecting my desires onto someone not actually interested? Could he be teasing me?

Biting my lip, I move past him and slide into the leather passenger seat. My nose wrinkles as the overpowering scent of winter pine air freshener cleanses out my sinuses.

When I get buckled in, my eyes flick to the time. *Shit.* I have a show in a couple of hours. Should I mention it? I really should be mentally prepping. I should be in my house writing songs and stressing about bills and wallowing in self-hatred.

Hail's fucking with my entire schedule.

When he slides in next to me, so close I can feel the warmth of his strong body, I forget everything but my desire to be touched by him.

After rummaging around, Hail retrieves a pair of sunglasses out of the centre console. He snorts. "You fucking prick. Armani sunglasses, Liam? Don't mind if I do." He slides them on and revs the engine. Then we're tearing down the gravel exit road like he's Dom from *Fast & The Furious* out for revenge.

He drums his fingers on the steering wheel as we approach the small market town of Melbourne where brick buildings nestle along the curving road we follow.

Coyly, Hail peeks over at me. "Shit. I feel like I should have asked for your consent or something. Do you consent to hanging out with me?"

I'm utterly speechless, still trying to figure out how to navigate this situation I've found myself in, and all because I had to see him again.

He wants to talk to me. He wants to spend time with me. Those thoughts send a little shiver of elation through me. The toxic part of my brain screams in response, *Shut it the fuck down. You have no right to ever feel this way again.*

"Z, can you verbalise something for me before I feel like a kidnapper? My brain is literally melting down after playing two shows in less than twenty-four hours." There's a hint of desperation in his tone, a contradiction to the confidence he exudes.

My brows shoot skyward. *I'm the one that paid 231 pounds to come stare at you in person.*

"I can. I do. I mean, yes. I want to be here," I stammer, fingers curling into my trousers over my thighs.

Good job, brain. Smooth.

His laugh is low and sensual, instantly jolting my dick awake. It strains against my zipper, and I adjust myself as soon as he looks out his side window for a second. This is rapidly spiraling out of control.

Hail whips us into a tight parking spot beside a cafe with broad windows and light blue painted trim. I trail him inside the eclectic shop, my features scrunched in utter confusion. The smell of roasted coffee beans and flaky pastries hit us, and Hail tips his head back, eyes closing on a groan. I run my tongue over my bottom lip as I imagine trailing my mouth up the column of his throat.

I break my gaze away before I'm left with a very visible boner I won't be able to fix in public.

This is not a date, dick. You hear me?

Heads turn toward us, anyway, because how could they not? Hail makes his own rules for the universe, and they include enslaving attention. Regardless of how good he looks, we're both dressed to make a scene, decked out in all black. My hair is the longest it's ever been, dark locks dangling into my eyes and around my ears.

Hail orders two teas, two bottles of water, and one of each dessert in the glass display case.

"For the band?" I inquire, watching the staff shove about a dozen different desserts into a paper bag.

"Hell no. They can buy their own stuff."

I fumble for my card, but he pushes it back into the slot in my wallet before I can fully remove it. Then he takes my wallet and reaches around to tuck it into my back pocket.

"My treat."

It's a quick move—he's a breath away, and then we're apart again—but I can't help the rush of warmth to my cheeks and neck at the thought of his hands on my body. Is he rough or gentle in bed, I wonder? How many lovers has he had? Probably more than I can count.

I clamp my teeth together. Okay, where in the good god fuck did those thoughts come from? Who's gatekeeping in my head right now?

My silence and awkward movements have to be an embarrassment for him as we gather up our drinks and treats. He guides us over to a corner table by the front windows in view of the car. When he sits across from me, he's wearing a comfortable smile, oblivious to the chaos I embody emotionally and physically.

Damn, he has such an addictive smile. It's worn in like he never travels without it.

He begins rifling through the bag with enthusiasm, setting out each dessert with a gleam of hunger in those stunning amber irises. "I've been wanting to hit up some cafes here. I swear this tour is going to be the death of me. Hope you don't mind that I ordered for us. I got a bit carried away."

"Um…" I shake my head. His gaze holds me, a flash of worry there. What does he see reflected back at him? Can he see the hole where my soul used to be? The splinters of my fractured heart?

Nothing he sees could be of worth.

I am nobody.

Panic starts to creep in, and my brain fumbles for an exit strategy. But then he reaches out to brush his calloused thumb over the back of my hand. My eyes shoot wide open, electricity sparking from the point of contact.

This time, Hail is the one to blush as he pulls his hand away, and my heart springs into action, bouncing around in my chest. "Sorry, couldn't resist. Your skin looks so soft. Is that a weird thing to say?" His hand raises to tug at his longer patch of hair, lifting it enough for me to glimpse the black and silver rings and delicate chains adorning his ear. "Don't answer that. It's weird as hell."

A soft laugh escapes me and we both relax into our chairs. "S'okay. I don't mind."

Boundaries, Z. Why are you not enforcing them?

His brilliant smile embraces me like a warm summer day. Drinking him in is better than sugar melting on my tongue. He's bliss personified. He's off fucking limits.

"So, was today a coincidence?" he asks, slouching in his chair as he bites into a mini bakewell tart.

I shift in my seat, tearing my gaze from his slightly pointed canines before twisted fantasies take over all brain function and cause me to erupt into flames.

Do I admit the truth? He's definitely caught me admiring him more than once now.

"Not exactly," I say, fingertips pressing into the tender spots beneath my kneecaps.

His head tilts in question, and he waits patiently for me to continue as he chews through a piece of sponge cake next. No way he can eat his way through all these desserts.

"I was… curious. Your skills are impressive."

"But." His tone is suddenly sharp.

Turning my attention fully back on him, I lift my hands in mock surrender. "Just stating a fact."

"But my lyrics are nothing like yours." He leans back in his chair once more, sucking each finger into his mouth to clean them. God, does he even realise what he's doing to me? How effortlessly sexy he is?

"I didn't say that." I shake my head a bit frantically. Did I offend him somehow? My brain cycles back through all of our interactions, seeking an answer and finding none. I've never been good at conversations, one of many reasons I usually try to avoid them.

"No. I am," Hail clarifies. "My lyrics are nothing like what you create. Liam agrees. You are raw talent. You're on another level, Z."

Nerves buzzing, I reach for the double chocolate cupcake as a distraction. His eyes dip to my mouth and linger there as I take a bite. My heart rate spikes as he reaches out to swipe his thumb over my bottom lip. He pulls it back, smeared in chocolate, and sucks this into his mouth, too.

I freeze. *Okay, dick. I can't be mad at you this time.*

He must be toying with me. There's no other explanation for what is happening. He picked up on my obvious lust and wanted to poke fun at the gay guy.

Cheeks heating, I focus my attention on finishing my cupcake, taking care not to get anymore on my face. If he touches me again, I think I might implode.

"Actually, I would love to collaborate with you. I've been playing around with the idea of a side project, and I would be lying if I said that you didn't make me feel something unforgettable that night in the bar."

My eyes dart back to him, jaw hanging open. "I'm… not sure if you're serious…"

"Why does no one think I can be serious?" He pouts for a second before popping an entire biscuit into his mouth.

Bloody hell, he's being sincere. My chest tightens with impending doom. How do I politely turn down someone of his caliber? If he takes this the wrong way, he has the power to tarnish my name in this industry forever. What artist would want to license my songs then?

On the other side of this scale, am I in the financial position to say no? Most of my savings went toward a funeral and putting my mum up in a place that would treat her. After years of circuiting Europe like a nomad, I'm down to the dredges of my bank account, the consequences of which would be dire for the only family member I have left to claim.

A side project with Hail would more than likely result in a steady paycheck. The guy's a powerhouse musician. The artistry we could create together...

"How would logistics work? Aren't you on tour?"

He shrugs. "A temporary hurdle, but we could always video chat. Pass things back and forth via email. Obviously, Atonement has to be my number one priority for a little while longer."

My brows furrow. Is he planning on leaving the band? There were rumors online about Liam retiring soon. Little side comments made in interviews.

I chew on my bottom lip. If I accept, *my* priority needs to stay locked on the money. I can't let temptation for the guy sitting two feet away from me lead me astray. That line cannot be crossed again. It's permanently etched in concrete.

"I honestly don't know what to say," I admit, dropping my eyes to the table.

He brushes crumbs aside and slides his phone toward me. "Say you'll at least consider it. Add your number. Then you can ask me all the questions you want. Or we can just chat." He offers a kind smile.

Breaths coming in shorter spurts, I blink down at his phone.

"Choice is one hundred percent yours, but I would really love to work with you. Maybe you can teach me how to summon something other than rage."

I can't help but grimace, which makes me feel guilty enough to punch in my number. What else am I supposed to do to extract myself painlessly from this situation? So what if he has my number? Doesn't mean I have to answer his calls or text him back. Soon he'll move on to another city and everything can go back to normal. I can go back to my secluded, pathetic life, and he can carry on wooing fans and building his reputation in the music industry.

He retrieves his phone. A few seconds later, my own phone vibrates in my pocket. I slip it out, my lungs expanding when I see his text. A smile emoji. You know, the one with hearts. Cute as fuck, and so at odds with surface-level Hail Koval.

"Thanks. I'll... uh... think about it. Though my process of making music lately hasn't been exactly... orthodox."

Meaning I haven't completed a song in weeks, too busy suffocating under the pressure of delivering so I can keep bills paid.

"I'm not into orthodox," Hail says, eyes glinting with a hint of mischief. "You ready?"

We leave the table, and Hail reaches back to slide his hand in mine. Simultaneously, blood rushes to my head and my crotch. I try to pull free, but he gives my hand a squeeze.

"If you're doing that for my sake, forget about it," he says softly. "I don't care what anyone thinks."

Stunned into silence, I quit fighting him. The question I've wondered since he let his eyes rove over me in Selma's bar sticks in my throat. I don't need to know the answer. Whatever this is, it can never be part of this collaboration—if I even decide to go through with it.

"Did you drive to the festival or catch a cab?" he asks, guiding me across the street to the Audi.

"Cab," I whisper, still floating from what just occurred and who it occurred with. What he offered me. Maybe a lifeline from the heavens. I can't blame medication today. I threw that up.

As we come to a stop at the passenger door, he drops my hand. His eyes move slowly over my features, but he gives me no further signs of interest. No neon blinking lights. Hail could be just an affectionate person by nature.

"Want me to drive you home?" he finally asks.

"Sure. I've got a gig in a few hours."

He flashes a smile. "Great, we can go together."

D id I expect to want to kiss him?

No.

But the desire was definitely there as I sat across from him in that cafe. Shockingly, more than a few times.

It's unavoidable, I guess. My attraction to Z is chemical. Visceral at the very center of my beating heart. Which is wading into foreign territory for me because I've never been into dudes. And I'm definitely not one to sign up for complicated relationships after what my ex put me through.

What I *was* expecting was the ability to exercise more self-control. The guy's obviously a runner. Pushes away any and all attention. If I'm going to win him over long enough to figure out if we vibe musically, I need to be more careful with my wandering eyes and hands.

With Z's quiet instruction, I pull into a tiny driveway between two old stone houses just outside of the city, one of which looks like it's survived at least a century. Maybe a couple of wars. Spiderweb cracks run through the mortar between dark rocks along its surface, and there's an overgrown garden in the back that looks jungle feral.

The cool thing about Europe is even when a place hasn't been well cared for, it still holds some kind of charm. History is soaked into the very foundation of these homes.

Z hesitates in the driveway after climbing out of the car. He runs a hand nervously up and down his long neck. My brain sticks on the idea of sinking my fingers into his lush, dark hair. I fiddle with the car keys instead, spinning them around my finger and catching them in my palm.

"Um, thanks for the ride. And for... the offer," he murmurs. "But you don't need to hang around. My set is the same tonight."

Warmth bleeds into my smile. "I don't mind. Cool if I chill?"

Alright. I'm acting crazy. Should I call Liam to drag me back to the festival and tie me down in the bus? I know he has bondage rope. Caught him with it when I drunkenly opened the connecting door between our hotel rooms to ask for a bottle of water late one night. Didn't question him or the naked female face down, ass up in his bed.

Though I did look at Liam in a new light the next morning. Not even a Texas-shaped waffle could ward off that awkward breakfast.

Z frowns. "Don't you... have better things to do?"

Oh no. I grip the keys tight in my palm. *He's too fucking cute.* The inward curve of his shoulders and the subtle bite of his full bottom lip and his mess of curls. He was designed to be my downfall. He is a test sent here by god. Do I give into temptation?

Play it cool. Don't mess this up.

"I can't think of a single thing I'd rather do than spend time with you," I reply foolishly.

His frown deepens, but he gives a little nod and leads me down the overgrown path between his house and a tall wooden privacy fence.

I can't deny it. I'm practically frothing at the mouth to peek into his life. To delve inside his creative mind. My phone buzzes in my pocket, but I ignore it. Probably just Liam or Sondra wondering where I ran off to.

I'm entitled to some privacy, damn it.

Z opens the front door, and my overactive heart begins to wither. While the landlord had enough decency to give the interior a fresh coat of off-white paint, really, it's just a mask for the layers of dirt and wear. Pretty sure there's a hole in one wall that was duct taped and painted.

Landlord's special, am I right?

I suppose if you keep your hands off the walls, it's a cozy enough space, even with the lack of furniture. There's a boxy gray couch situated against the wall opposite from a small mounted TV. Shoved in a tiny room better served as a closet, I spot a messy desk, two guitars, and a radiator. The kitchen at the back of the house is nothing more than a galley ending in glass doors to the backyard. Down a short hallway, I glimpse a small bathroom and a bedroom with a mattress on the floor. Unlike the rest of the house, which is nearly untouched, Z's bedroom is a tornado of tangled bedsheets and bunched up clothes.

He rushes over to shut the bedroom door. "Kind of a mess," he admits, pink staining his lovely cheekbones.

For once, I can't force a smile. "How long have you lived here?"

I don't know what I expected. More artwork and color and life, maybe? Some rowdy roommates, possibly students enrolled in a graduate music program that balance out Z's quiet nature like Malek, Griff, and I do with Liam? Shit, maybe even a cat he pretends to hate but actually cuddles with in bed at night?

His home is depressingly vacant, the silence nearly deafening.

Sucking in a breath, Z hurries over to the kitchen. He shoves a handful of prescription bottles into the cabinet above the stove, and my chest tightens into painful little knots.

I barged in here. Dragged him onto the tour bus, and then to that cafe. Invited myself to his home and to his performance this evening. Forced an offer upon him to see if we fit musically. And, if I'm being honest, maybe in other ways, too.

Clearly, Z's stressed about my presence here. No one has accused me of being considerate. Hell, I've always been able to do what I please without much consequence. Not that I've ever done anything bad.

"Um, just over a month. I tend to roam otherwise," he says, ruffling the hair over his forehead.

I nod, hoping to appear nonchalant when I just want this tightness between my lungs to go away. More than that, I don't want to see him embarrassed.

Turning to his desk, I leap at the opportunity to sweep up both guitars. *Music is safe. We don't even need to talk.*

I bring them over to the couch, holding out his acoustic guitar while I keep his black Stratocaster, more in line with what I'm used to playing on stage.

Z's clenched muscles visibly uncoil. He wanders over and rests his guitar on his lap. With his timid gaze on me, I take the lead and begin to play. My pulse quickens as he matches my chords effortlessly. Our musical union is everything I believed it would be. A dream I don't want to wake from.

I break away from the melody we've created, letting my fingers dance across the fret in show. It's an energetic riff, powered by my determination to take on the weight of his wounded spirit and lift it up and up. I want to hang it from the stars where it belongs. He sang about wings the other night, and I want to show him what it's like to soar.

Peeking up at him, I can't contain my toothy smile. There's a spark in his pale eyes. Oh yeah, he's feeling this chemistry, too. I've played with hundreds of musicians over the years. Heard plenty more during our climb to fame.

None hold a candle to Z's ability to draw out emotion. He pours everything into his performance. His fingers move fluidly, plucking and sliding and bending. The little sway of his head and the way his eyelids grow heavy have me in a trance.

You're beautiful, the words play on my lips. I clench my jaw tight to keep them locked away.

We fall back into sync, and then Z's the one to take me for a journey, drawing me into a slow, swampy, chugging tune with roots in old country.

My laugh is breathy. "See? We could be so good together."

He flushes, head dipping to hide his features. The moment hits me all at once, like a camera zooming into a set. Us alone in his house. How close we've positioned ourselves on the couch. His knee pressed against mine. My heart beating out of rhythm as if I just finished a two-hour performance.

Rising first, I drift into the small room where I found his instruments. As I prop his Stratocaster against the wall, I take in the unorganized chaos. Strewn, wrinkled paper, bits of eraser and pencil shavings. There are divots carved down to the particle board in his desk by what looks like fingernails.

My stomach churns as Z sneaks by me to gather up the papers before I can decipher the scribbled writings. "Those aren't... finished," he says, pain embedded in his words.

Leaning back against the wall, I tuck my hands in my pockets to keep from touching anything else. Mostly him. I turn my solemn gaze to him. "I'm sure they're all perfect."

His wide eyes meet mine. Languidly, he takes in my features, lingering on my mouth as his throat bobs. *Definitely interest there.*

But the flicker of panic on his face warns me against crossing that line. I shove down the urge to take him into my arms and comfort him. I'm willing to take this slow. Take our time figuring out whatever the fuck is happening between us, because I don't think I've ever felt this consumed by anyone before.

He blows out a soft breath before slipping out of the room, breaking the charged tension between us. Suddenly, I'm overwhelmed by the sense that I'm encroaching on his solitude.

Bones leaden with disappointment, I head for the front door. "I'll leave you to get ready for your show. You have my number. Call or text if you decide you're interested in working together or want to go out and get another tea while I'm still in town."

Granting myself one more glance back at him, I catch him tugging on the ends of his sweater sleeves. He nods, and it takes every fiber of my will to leave him alone.

Why do I have the sinking feeling I'm never going to see him again?

Six

I'm more than a little distracted on stage.

Not just because of the whirlwind of an afternoon I just experienced—I haven't processed any of that beyond scouring the internet to make sure pictures from the cafe where Hail Koval held my hand didn't make headlines.

That's the last thing he needs in the prime of his fame. To be outed publicly, regardless of where his romantic preferences actually lie. Worse, to be spotted engaging with someone like me. There would be another attempt to uncover who I am. What makes me tick. Why I vanished. What horrible things I did.

It would ruin Hail's reputation in an instant.

In addition to these nightmarish thoughts, I'm horrified by the size of the crowd in Selma's bar tonight. My eyes cut to her in the middle of a song, right as she tosses her head back with wild laughter at something her customers have told her.

Is this a result of Atonement's visit a few nights ago? Did it get leaked that they'd been lurking around the underground bar scene? Has Selma figured me out and used the knowledge to her advantage to increase her business?

I don't need the attention. Don't want it. Even when I was centre stage for Visage, I kept my hood up and a mask over the lower half of my face, always satisfied to keep to the shadows.

Who would have thought that would only drive fans to be more curious about my identity? You would think they would respect the fact that I wanted to remain anonymous. So far, I have, but there were so many attempts to uncover who I was. Where I was from. If I was single. If I was hiding an ugly mug beneath the mask.

Can we just fast forward this weekend so Atonement can ship off to another festival and direct their charm at other people without a laundry list of problems?

That's what Hail deserves, after all. Someone normal. Someone whole.

His pained expression has lurked behind my closed eyes since he practically bolted out of my house. I haven't heard from him since, and he hasn't shown up tonight.

It's exactly what I wanted, right? So why do I feel so... unhinged? Like I've forgotten something important? Or like I'm just waking up from a strange dream after five years of slumber?

Focus on your finances, Z. Your life is falling apart, and that affects other people's lives, too.

It's weeks before I'll get another royalty check, and I owe the facility that treated my mum a substantial amount of pounds.

Which brings me to the song of the night. New material I wrote after Hail backpedaled out of my life. A song I'm nearly ready to hand over to an artist that has been patiently waiting for me to produce something of worth.

Our demons cross paths and take aim, eager for the slaughter
Will we both survive this?
Will we ever have the chance to hold each other?
Or will we be haunted by shadows forever?

Washed up rockstar doesn't even begin to describe me. I never actually got to ride that wave of fame. I had a big label contract in hand, but instead of being responsible and reading over it with the band, we celebrated prematurely.

The damage done that night can never be erased.

I haven't talked with Eric or Jackson since I fled town shortly after. Out of morbid curiosity, I looked them up about four years ago. They'd both joined separate bands, off on lengthy tours in the United States. Eric had even gotten married to his private school sweetheart, and they were expecting their first kid.

If I even catch a whisper of your existence, I will deliver a world of hurt to your doorstep. You're a selfish piece of shit, Zander. You're worthless. You're nobody.

Jackson's text is still on my phone. I can't bring myself to delete it or remove his number, though he's definitely changed it by now.

Forcing my attention back on the ball of wretched emotions expanding in my chest, I start in on a slower song. Melodic notes ring out from my acoustic guitar, filling the dimly lit bar.

My set ends with an outburst of shouts and clapping, more than I've received before, and it rightly freaks me the fuck out. Do they know? How long before Jackson shows up at my house to rip me apart? To tear into all the wretched things I've kept barricaded away for five long years?

I'm trembling with so much fear and adrenaline and mental exhaustion that I zip up my guitar and bolt out of the emergency exit in the back of the bar, spilling into an alleyway.

As soon as the heavy door shuts and locks behind me, I let out a frustrated growl. I need those tips from Selma, but I can't summon up the courage to walk back in there and face the crowd. The very thought has my pulse throbbing and my lungs constricting.

My head hangs heavy on my neck. This might be the last time I can perform here without drawing up some suspicion. Selma might even be grateful to be rid of me.

I tug my hood up and start the five-mile walk home, down ghost-silent streets and out into the countryside on a narrow, paved road lined by rocky walls and fields of tall grasses. Sheep bleat at me and bounce away. Even they can't stand my company, and I don't blame them.

I don't bother turning on the lights when I get home. There's a missed call from mum's health institute on my phone, and a text from one of the artists that contracted me to deliver a few hits. The songs sit unfinished on my desk.

I toss my phone on them and go sit in the shower. Fully clothed, I run the water ice cold until my body goes completely numb.

"Y'all are blowing up on social media, bro!" Stasi cheers, her cell bobs in her hand as she jogs the wooded trail around her apartment complex in Dallas. Her long, blonde ponytail swings behind her head, fed through the hole in the back of her Cowboys hat.

I force a wide grin as I plop down on the leg press machine in our hotel gym. I've made it four whole hours without thinking about Z since I left his run-down countryside house. "Really? That's fucking wild!"

Her eyes narrow as she finally glances down at the camera. "How do you not know this? Don't you interact with your fans?"

"I would, but I think it'd give me too big of a head. Next thing you know, I'll be referring to myself in third person and asking you to erect a shrine in my name."

After obsessively checking the internet for stats when our first album dropped, I quickly realized this habit was a) not healthy, b) not going to increase our sales, and c) not going to convince my parents or older brother that I'd made the right choice quitting high school to pursue music.

The latter is still an open wound, but it probably will be forever. No matter how much we're appreciated by our fans or how the media spins us, I'm still that southern boy with a gnawing ache for his family's support.

"I'm so proud of you, Hail," Stasi says, feeding me exactly what my soul hungers for. Leave it to my twin to read my mind. Though we're not identical, our brains are synced up like we're one operating system. "You've worked hard to get to where you're at."

I groan. "Damn it, Stasi. You know I can't be seen crying at the gym. Liam will make sure I can't walk for a week."

She swipes at a rogue tear and adjusts her baseball cap. "I'm the one crying, dork."

"Yeah, but if you cry, then I cry. We're like the same person."

Liam strolls passed to rest his massive dumbbells on the rack by the wall of mirrors. He gives me a long look with a cocked brow.

"How are classes going?" I ask. "You have to be close to finishing, right?"

It's enough of a shift in conversation to shut down the waterworks. I rarely cry, but when I do, it's never-ending. Really, the dramatics are impressive.

Stasi rolls her eyes. "Ugh. Tough. Between physical therapy courses and my internship, there's no light at the end of the tunnel. Tell me why you let me party my early twenties away and switch my major three times? I'll be in college forever at this rate, drowning in debt."

"You've got this. You're on track to graduate in the spring."

But my smile wavers. Even through all of Stasi's irresponsible decision-making, somehow I ended up the fuck-up by not pursing a secondary education and following my dad and Max into business.

"You still have that crazy roommate? The one that let her cat eat all of your granola bars?" I ask with a chuckle.

"God no! She got fired for having sex with a patient at her clinic. She moved out weeks ago."

This grabs Liam's attention mid-stroke on the rowing machine. Sometimes, I get the sense that he wants me to hand the phone over so he can talk with Stasi with the way he tunes into our conversations. He rarely gets phone calls, so I give him a pass.

"Nope, it's just me for now." She sighs, lips pursing. "I'm going to see if I can swing rent alone."

"I can send you money—"

"Hail, I swear." Her voice takes on more of a southern twang. One day, she will entice fear into the hearts of her children with her no-nonsense tone. "If you so much as Cash App me a dime, I will never forgive you."

"I just don't want you under Mom and Dad's roof again. It's not healthy," I counter. Noticing my slacking, Liam leans over to move the pin on the weights down a few notches.

Hate you, I mouth at him.

He gives me a wink. If I wasn't confident he'd lay me out on the floor, I'd jump on his back like a rabid spider monkey.

"Seriously, though." I grunt through a few leg presses, relishing in the burn. "I'm not there to take the edge off all their overbearing judgment. Don't get me started on the passive-aggressive mutterings from Dad."

Stasi slows to a walk. "You're not a human punching bag for me, Hail."

"Just promise me you'll let me know first if you get into a rough situation, okay?"

"I'm not promising shit. I'm a grown ass woman. I'll figure out my own problems."

I glimpse Liam cracking a smile at that, and a flicker of anger works through my chest. That hall pass to listen in on me and Stasi's conversations is nearing expiration.

"I'm two minutes older," I try to argue.

Liam and Stasi both snort.

"Is that Liam? Tell him to make you hurt. I gotta run, big bro. Quite literally. Love you!" She drags out the last word like she's done since we were kids.

"Love you, too, Stasi."

The instant we hang up, Liam puts me through the wringer. I'm left gasping and dripping sweat, regretting my moment of weakness when I asked him to whip me into shape after devouring a basket of chips at the attached pub.

And still, the burn of too many reps isn't enough of a distraction.

Before I pocket my phone, I check through my messages just in case Z decided to reach out. *Nothing*. It shouldn't summon dread to my gut, but it does. I can't help my worry for him. My inability to shut down this need to care for others definitely isn't genetic. It was a learned behavior growing up in a toxic environment.

Weights aren't doing shit to clear my mind. Obviously, I need to push myself more. I need to punish every muscle in my body so I can actually sleep tonight. We have one more day of rest in London, and then we're on the road to Paris.

Moving over to the treadmill, I stuff in my wireless headphones, then I crank up the speed. I keep my pulse throttled to the max, metal blasting in my ears, hoping to burn off this weird prickling anxiety surfacing in me. That unsettling itch I get when I'm taunted with something new and shiny and consuming and in need of fixing.

I want to text him.

I shouldn't text him.

I scared him away. Came on too strong.

If he's interested, he'll reach out.

The heavy metal vibrating my skull isn't loud enough, and this damn treadmill isn't going fast enough, and fuck if I don't just want to check in on him, even if he doesn't want to make music together.

My finger smashes down on the speed button. I'm typing out a message to him before I slow to a walk.

Hey, it's Hail. You know, from Atonement.

Should I scratch that last sentence? I don't want to come off pretentious. Before I can second guess myself, I hit the send button and wait, aware of Liam's eyes darting over to me as I check my phone a dozen times.

After twenty minutes of no response, a heavy sigh escapes me. "I'm beat," I mumble, hitting the stop button on the treadmill and wiping a towel across my sweaty face.

Liam gives a nod. "Catch you in the morning."

There's a buzz from my phone in the pocket of my gym shorts. A surge of excitement floods my body. Gripping my phone tightly in my hand, I hurry out the gym door and read over the message from Z in privacy.

Hi Hail from Atonement.

My heart flutters. He responded. What could that mean? Either he's interested or he pities me, right? God, you better give me the answers, or I'll be tempted to slingshot myself up to heaven and shake them out of you.

I type out another message as I get into the elevator and mash the button for my floor.

How did your performance go?

Better than expected, thanks.

Glad to hear it.

When I get nothing back from him, I flop down on my hotel bed. Is he mad that I didn't show up? It didn't really seem like he wanted me there. Or anywhere near him, to be honest.

Heartbeat accelerating, I type out another message. *Sorry I didn't come. I assumed you needed space away from me breathing down your neck.*

Three dots pop up, hover there for a minute, then disappear. I squeeze my eyes shut and try to reason through why I'm so upset by his silence. Because I've known him all of a few days, and I'm already in too deep. Because I had hope. Because I've been hurt before. Because I give my all to everyone and everything, and it's never enough.

I'm never enough.

I end up falling asleep, cradling my phone over phantom pains in my chest where my heart was once ripped out by cruel hands.

EIGHT

Z

I wake up, all 1.9 metres of my gangly body cramped on the wet shower floor, sicker than a fucking dog. My skin is on fire, despite the cold droplets splattering up at me from the ricochet of the waterspout.

Groaning, I reach an arm up and shut off the icy water. My clothes are completely drenched, hair plastered to my throbbing skull.

Why do I do shit like this? Further sink myself into trouble when I'm already barely passing as a human being?

Like a monster from the black lagoon, I crawl out of the shower, my fitted trousers and long-sleeve shirt squishing from the amount of water they've absorbed. I snatch my phone off the bathroom tiles and check the time.

Eight in the morning. Last time I checked, it was just after three A.M. That means my water has been running for five solid hours. Dread curdles in my gut at the thought of opening the next notice from my landlord. She'll definitely cut me off.

There's a text message from Hail that I failed to answer last night before passing out. My heart thuds painfully at his apology, but I know I need to keep him at a distance. I have to fight against this urge to delve into whatever he thinks he needs from me.

I have nothing good to offer him.

After dragging my aching body into my bedroom to change into dry clothes, I saunter into the living room and find a hand-written notice shoved under the front door.

My stomach churns. Yeah, I'd say my landlord is pretty pissed off over the fact that my first month's rent check bounced. I log into my bank account on my phone and sigh in defeat. Of course it's in the negative.

How do I explain to my landlord that all of my royalties are going toward my mum's bills and that she'd rather lie down in oncoming traffic than have me step foot in her house again? That I was too daft and strung out at the time to set up a will for my brother's quid, never imagining I'd lose him so young. That mum would blow through his savings without a care, demanding I fund the funeral because everything was my fault.

Even if she would accept me back into her life, I don't think I can step foot in that house without being haunted.

Gripping the ends of my hair, I run through my options. Pick up a side job and hope some other landlord will overlook my piss-poor payment history when I get evicted from this place. Ask to crash on Selma's couch until I can finish the damn songs I owe artists. Find more local scenes to perform at, ignoring the fact that I spiral out pretty hardcore afterward. Admit defeat and hole up in my bathroom until my landlord calls the police to physically rip me from shelter.

The gnawing emptiness in my stomach becomes priority number one. No one should have to make a difficult decision while hungry.

I scrounge through the musty kitchen cabinets with sluggish limbs. How can my body feel like I'm roasting under a heat lamp when I spent a chunk of my night drenched in cold water?

Discovering a package of noodles, I boil and season them until they no longer smell like cardboard. Then I polish them off, slurping down the salty broth.

Fuck. I'm still hungry.

My head drops down to rest on my dining table as my fingers pick at the edges of the late notices that have started multiplying, the one I just received this morning from my landlord, along with the others I refuse to open. Doesn't matter what they say inside, I can't pay them.

How did things get so fucked up? Five years ago, I would have laughed if someone told me this is what my life would turn into. Only, I'm one hundred percent to blame for my situation. Nothing's going to change the fact that my brother's dead and my mum's life crumbled, thanks to *my* selfish decisions.

While I sometimes toss around the idea of dying, it would leave mum high and dry. Death may be a solution to my problems, but it's not a settlement for the debt of pain I still owe.

Which leads me back to my need to acquire income.

I pick up my phone. With shaking fingers, I type out a message to Hail Koval, asking how we could make things work. What this collaboration might look like. The buzz of a phone call startles me a second after his read notification pops up in our chat.

"Hey!" Hail answers, out of breath. The fucked up part of my brain convinces me that he was in the middle of sex. What else do metal gods do in their spare time except seek pleasure? Man or woman, the visual of his exquisitely toned body thrusting makes my already overheated body flood with desire.

"Z? You there?" he asks, a note of worry in his tone.

"Hey." My voice is barely audible when I croak out an answer. "Look, I'm... I'm not promising anything..."

If I could be honest with him, I'd explain that I'm not in the proper mental state to accept work from anyone right now. I *should* keep my distance, but as long as we keep things professional, I think I can survive a few songs together. I'll have to be clear that our partnership is temporary.

"Are you home? Can I pick you up to chat?" Hail asks eagerly.

I slide my nail along the corner of an envelope. It slices the tender skin underneath, and I watch as a tiny bead of red appears. "I'm actually pretty sick, I think."

The admission burns in my throat, but if anything will keep a vocalist away, it's the threat of catching a bug.

His silence picks at me.

"Hang on," he murmurs, and I hear keys jingling in the background. "I'll be there in thirty minutes."

Hail leaves no room for argument as the line clicks, and my head spins, my fever digging in with fiery rage.

For the first time since I met Z, there's a real prickle of worry that I might be in over my head with him. Red flags wave as I burst through his unlocked front door when he doesn't answer my reckless banging.

I find his upper body laid out on his dining room table. Panic slingshots me toward him, and I don't hesitate to put my hands on him. His forehead is coated in a sheen of sweat, and his eyes are sealed shut.

My first thought is to ask if he needs any of the medication he shoved away in the cabinet yesterday. Does he have a medical condition? Or did he really just catch a bug?

While I should be concerned about my health, only because everyone on the tour relies on each other to come to work ready to perform, I can't help but drop down to my knees so I can get a better look at him.

"Z?" I push back locks of his damp hair and lay my palm against his sticky cheek. "Jesus, you're burning up."

His eyes remain closed. "If I move, I might vomit."

"That's okay. I'm here now. We'll get you fixed up, I promise."

Sadness rushes through me as I glimpse the past due notices beside his head. Is he having financial problems? With the way he writes lyrics, he shouldn't have an issue licensing songs. Hell, I'm willing to pay any amount to get my hands on his work.

Regardless, I can't sign off on him staying here alone in this condition. Like a nun on a holy mission, I ransack his bedroom for clean clothes. I find a backpack in his barren closet and shove clothes into it. I don't bother with bathroom items. Those are replaceable. The hotel we're staying at should have whatever he needs, and if not, I'll find a store to run to. I neatly tuck his loose songs into a notebook and slip that inside the bag as well.

There's no complaining from him as I overstep boundaries. No inclining that he's going to lash out or bite me. He seems willing to accept my help, and I'm more than willing to give it.

Stasi used to tease me that I should have become a nurse. If I hadn't found music and allowed it to possess me, I might have pursued a career in caring for others.

Moving to the kitchen, I search for a bottle of water or something for him to drink on the way back into town. He needs fluids. But when I crack open the fridge, I find it nearly empty.

"Geez, remind me to bring you some groceries next time."

"I'm not a charity case," he mutters weakly.

My brows furrow. "No, I know that. I didn't mean it that way. Just figured maybe you were too busy to bother with shopping."

He lets out a heavy sigh. "Sorry. Trying my best not to be me."

Running a hand down my face, I motion to the cabinet with medicine. "Do you need anything from there?"

"No," he forces the word out, closing his eyes. "Nothing helps."

True fear grips my insides. Swallowing, I nod and move on. "Do you have family nearby? Anyone I can call?"

That probably should have been my first question before barging into his life again. Who am I to assume he even wants me taking care of him?

"No. There's nobody."

I'm not an angry person by nature, but I'm up in fucking arms, ready to launch into action. Against what enemy, I don't know. I'm keyed up over the state Z has been left in.

When I was first introduced to Liam's darkness, the pain he harbored, I realized just how monstrous blood relatives could be. Did someone hurt Z, too? Why is he alone?

Slipping the backpack over my shoulder, I return to his side. "I'm going to take you back to our hotel so we can keep an eye on that fever. Anything else you need?"

The fact that he hasn't questioned me about packing up his shit means he's got to be well out of it. How can I let him ride this out by himself, though? What if he needs to see a doctor? Needs antibiotics?

I know Liam and Sondra, our manager, would be furious if I camped out here until we're due to hit the road again.

I normally wouldn't complain about the fast pace of a tour. This is the longest break we've had between shows since we hit the European circuit, but it's not enough time to assure Z's back on his feet.

"You don't need to bother," Z replies, seeming to dissolve further into the table.

"You don't know me very well, then. Come on, up you go." I peel him off the wooden surface. His skin burns against my own, his body radiating desert heat. Should I take him to urgent care? I'm not even sure if they have those here. I've never had to seek out medical treatment in another country.

Hotel first. Sondra will know what to do.

Tires screech as I pull into the parking lot in Liam's rented Audi. As soon as we enter the sprawling lobby, Sondra's already there, pacing with her phone in hand. Her fiery red hair is pulled taut in a high ponytail, and she's dressed in her usual pantsuit battle armor.

"Where the hell did you run off to again?" she scolds, eyeing me like I've just dragged in a problem.

My mouth turns down. *He's a very cute problem, though*, I want to argue.

"I... um, made a friend in town, and he's very sick," I reply.

"A friend. A *sick* friend." Sondra's glare cuts through me like an x-ray. She's always been more aware of my thoughts and emotions than I'm comfortable with. I suppose that's what makes her a good manager. Which is why I've put so much effort into avoiding her lately, not wanting to give away my unrest over the future of the band when Liam retires.

"Sorry for the trouble," Z murmurs.

Between his pathetic state and my pleading expression, Sondra curses under her breath and helps guide him up to my hotel room. We lay him out on my bed. Instantly, her mom instincts take over as she rests a hand against his forehead. "How long have you had a fever?"

"Few hours," he mumbles. "Barely got any sleep. Fell asleep in the shower. Water ran cold."

Sondra sighs, and I try to suppress the frustration bubbling in my gut. Why did he share that with her and not me? Does he not trust me? Or is Sondra working some mom voodoo magic to draw truths from within against his will?

"Well, let's hope you're not contagious," she says, throwing me another rage-filled look. "Hail should have taken you to a medical center first."

I throw out my arms. "I don't know how that shit works here."

"Call someone. Google it. What are you, an infant? Scratch that, I know you are. All of you are." She shakes her head like she's trying to rid her brain of years of being on tour with us.

My hand snaps over my chest. "You wound me."

She's about to fire back with more heat when Z mumbles, "No doctor."

My anger fades as I catch him snuggling deeper into the pillow, eyes shut and body finally at ease. I can't argue with him like this. If he's content to sleep off this fever in my bed, who am I to deny him that comfort?

"I have a meeting with our booking agent and promoters in ten minutes. You should get him some fluids and Tylenol," Sondra instructs, rising from the edge of the bed. "We're going to have a conversation later, Hail. And you need to let the others know you have a guest so they don't barge in here and scare the living daylights out of him. Malek and Griff have been on the hunt for you. They're on edge thinking you're going to follow your work wife into early retirement."

"Got it." I give her a salute, burying my guilt, which earns a snort of disgust. "You're the best, Sondra. Don't work too hard."

She leaves us, and I lean down to run a hand over Z's silky hair. "Will you be okay if I run to the drugstore? I'll make Olympic time, I swear."

He nods. As if bitten by something, he leans up and reaches for the hem of his shirt to drag it off. "Sorry, I'm on fucking fire."

"You want to cool off in the shower?" I ask.

"No," he snaps back. "This is good. Unless you don't want me sweating on your bed. I can move."

I hiss through my teeth, my masochistic brain flooding me with images of Z naked and writhing in pleasure on my sheets, my body pinning him down as I work my cock inside of his perfect little hole.

"Don't you dare move," I order, helping him drag his tight pants off as well. Stripped down, he sprawls his tall, lean body over the comforter. I hover over him long enough to assure he doesn't need anything more than the two bottles of water I set on the nightstand.

Alright, I get Sondra's point about informing the others. The band would hound me with questions if they barged in here now and found a half-naked guy in my bed. And admitting to them what I'm actually doing with Z, pursuing a musical connection, would be way worse than fessing up to my attraction to him.

Not that the band would care. But I haven't shown interest in anyone in years.

"Can you grab my phone and text Selma? No performances this weekend," he mumbles.

My brows raise. "Of course."

I slip his phone out of his pants, bunched on the floor. *No fucking security lock. Oh, Z.* I scroll through the eight contacts he has in confusion. I can't help but notice he has over a hundred missed calls too, which is worrisome as fuck for the small amount of numbers he has stored. I text myself Selma's contact information, then I hit the call button on my phone as I stroll out of the hotel room in pursuit of drugstore supplies.

"Who the hell is this?" Selma answers.

I chuckle. "Goodness, you're frightening. It's Mykhail Koval with Atonement. Z asked me to give you a call. He's out of commission this weekend."

"Is he in trouble?" Her voice is strained, and I'm thankful Z has at least one caring person in his life, whether he realizes it or not.

"He's safe with me. Should I notify anyone else about him coming down with a bug?"

There's a long pause on the other end. "Z's probably going to kill me for this, but I haven't even admitted to him that I've figured him out. You have to promise me you won't tell him I was the one that let the cat out of the bag."

Worry sluices through my veins. "Okay. He isn't like... a mass murderer or something, right? Please don't tell me I put my band in that kind of trouble."

Sondra isn't even phased by my question. "Do you remember Visage? They hit the music industry hard about five years ago."

"Shit, yeah. They were about to make it big, and then they fell off the face of the planet."

Liam and I used to fanboy over their djent breakdowns, well-written lyrics, and masked identities...

"Oh, fuck," I utter, hand tugging at the longer tendrils of my hair. I mean, Z's good. But there's *no* way. Muting the phone, I click into Google and search for images of the lead vocalist. With his oversized black hoodie and bandana with a skeleton design covering his nose and mouth, it would be hard for anyone to determine his identity, but I recognize those dark curls and unmistakable iceberg eyes.

It feels like a dirty secret discovering him this way. Forcing myself to breathe in and out, I switch back over to my conversation with Selma. "Why are you telling me this?"

"Because the last time he skipped out on collecting tips, I didn't see him for two years. You managed to earn his trust enough to get my number, which I've threatened him against handing out. There was quite a fuss about his disappearance years ago. I'm not sure why he's still hiding, but just take care with him. Don't mention you know who he is."

A potent mixture of curiosity and guilt battle for dominance in my head. I crave more truths about Z, but I can respect his privacy, especially when I know how precious that can be. Almost everything I do is blasted out into the limelight.

Just thinking about how detrimental it would be if it got leaked that I was questioning my position in Atonement has me determined to keep Z's secret. To protect him. How betrayed would Malek and Griff feel? They've been like brothers to me. And Sondra and the crew? My decision would affect all of them.

Not to mention the fans. Would they be disappointed? Or would they understand? Would they allow me space to explore music in other ways? Or am I fated to forever hold the title of metal god and nothing more?

"Thanks for trusting me," I say when Selma asks if I've hung up on her. "You're still my favorite Brit."

I catch her calling me a kiss arse right as the phone cuts off.

Once my basket at the drugstore is filled with Gatorade and medicine—thanks to the pharmacist's detailed rundown of options after I gave him an autograph and a picture—I check out. Then I swing by a Mediterranean restaurant to purchase soup, vegetables, and grilled chicken.

To my frustration, Liam catches me strolling through the hotel lobby. He's dressed down in navy cargo pants and a form-fitting gray henley, his dark hair half twisted up into a knot. He's unnaturally good at the laid back sexy look. It's criminal, really.

"Hey," he calls out, tipping his chin up. "We're all headed out to get some grub. You coming?"

I lift my bags, and his eyes narrow at the contents. "Got plans tonight. Next time for sure."

He shrugs off the questions I see swirling in his dark gaze, never one to judge when he's got a random stranger in his room almost every night of the week.

A little wave of nerves washes over me. What will Liam think when he realizes who I'm hiding away? I know Sondra told me to inform the others about Z, but I can do that when they get back from dinner. If I told them now, Griff and

Malek might be tempted to crawl into bed with Z to dissect him with a thousand questions. Z needs sleep.

Returning to my hotel room, I place the food and groceries on the table and wander over to the side of the king bed. My chest tightens as I listen to the sound of Z's gentle snores. I'm not really sure what the fuck I'm doing or why I'm not being as open as I normally am with the others. Chalk it up to a mid-life crisis or something.

But part of me doesn't want to give this a label just yet, no matter the undeniable weight of it in my life. My brain is still trying to figure out what I want. How my future will look when Liam's no longer on tour with us.

And the other part fears judgment. What if the others don't understand my choices? I've chased approval for so long; how do I handle shifting gears now?

Perching on the side of the bed, I work to delicately tie up half of Z's hair to keep it off his forehead like Stasi used to do for me when I was sick and our mom couldn't be bothered. She always had too many obligations at the country club or with her bunko group.

Retrieving a cool cloth from the bathroom, I brush it against his flawless skin, drawing it down the length of his elegant neck. He moans, cracking an eye open. Seemingly satisfied with what he sees, he closes his eye once more.

"Am I dead?" His question is muffled by the fluffy pillow.

"You're not dead." My hand tightens on the cloth, one finger extending to trace a lovely curl behind his ear. Goosebumps raise on his skin. "If you were, I would break down heaven's gates to bring you back down to earth with me."

I can't help that I'm mostly heart. It's a blessing and a curse.

His silence twists my gut, warning me that I overstepped again.

"Am I high?" he finally asks.

Stomach twisting into little knots, I recall all the prescription bottles in his kitchen cabinet. "Did you take something, Z?"

I've watched drugs ruin too many other bands over the years. If he's addicted to something... Jesus, I don't know what I'd do. Call up an army of professional help to guide him through it? Whatever the most extreme reaction is sounds about right for me.

"No. Just wondering how you can be real."

My gentle laugh relieves the worry my brain was spinning like a cotton candy machine operated by a clown with something to prove. I hold a cup of Night Nurse medicine to his lips. "You have weird brands here. Thankfully, the pharmacist was a fan of Atonement and helped me pick shit out. I paced the aisles for a good ten minutes. People thought I was insane."

He leans up just enough to drink down the green liquid, then flops back down on the bed.

Sighing, I tuck our meal in the fridge. Then I grab the bag of weird Twizzlers I bought and settle into the bed next to him to wait out his sickness.

My eyes adjust to a dark, unfamiliar room.

Terror has me rising up on a forearm, the sensation of warm blood seeping over my body lingering from another nightmare. I glance around and spot white light shining from under a hotel bathroom door. The rhythmic sound of water striking tile filters through the ambulance sirens slowly fading in my ears.

I fight to remember where I am and how I got here. It wouldn't be the first time I've blacked out on something and wound up in a dangerous situation.

But then I remember Hail's gentle touches. His fingers ruffling my hair. His encouraging words to drink more fluids throughout the day and night. His soft laughter as he tuned into some comedy show on TV. The comfort of his body lined up against mine in the bed, knees and hips and elbows touching, like we've known each other intimately for years.

My cheeks flood with surprising heat. Despite what fans and the media may believe about Mykhail Koval, the guy's a softie. He spent his precious free time tending to me. I don't know that there's an ounce of malice in his bones. He's considerate and talented and... tempting as hell.

Rubbing at my eyes, I push off the bed without any ache in my muscles. No urge to puke, either. My throat feels fine too, and I wonder if I dreamed up being sick. How fucking long was I out?

I wander over to the curtains and pull one side back enough to hiss at the bright sunlight that assaults me. Either I passed out for a couple hours or for an entire day. Judging by the way I feel, I'm leaning toward the latter.

Shutting the curtains once more, I flick on a lamp and find my backpack propped in a chair. Hail must have packed it for me. I can't help a smirk as I look through the random selections he made. No matching socks, but at least he managed to find a clean pair of boxers.

My chest tightens. I know I should keep my walls up to protect Hail from the damage I cause, but I'm also appreciative of everything he's done. It's more than anyone's done for me since Lex...

Fuck. My fingers dig into the textured material of my backpack. I can't go there right now.

I swallow down the expanding ball of emotions in my throat. Fighting the urge to claw at my skin or self-medicate, I pull out my notebook and plop down in a chair, not bothering with a shirt, to work through half a song before Hail walks out of the bathroom, wrapped in only a towel.

Whatever parameters I've set for myself when it comes to the metal god are demolished in an instant. I'm in rapture over his exposed skin. It's sun-kissed and smooth. I want to run my hands over his defined strength. Stroke a fingertip along the bars speared through his pink nipples. Trace the lines of the intricate, black and white dueling Chinese dragons up the side of his body, highlighted by golden flowers.

He catches me blatantly checking him out and flashes a seductive grin. "Feeling better, I see."

Nodding, I rip my attention away from his body and stare at the ink in my notebook. "Felt a moment of inspiration after your excellent care. You didn't have to do any of this. Thank you, though."

He moves closer, leaning down to wrap an arm loosely around my neck. It's a half embrace, one that brings his scent of rain and spicy body wash into my lungs where I want to trap it forever.

"Anytime, Z. Anytime."

He pulls away and rifles through a suitcase for clothes while I distract myself, sketching little designs along the margins in my notebook to keep from watching him dress.

"Do I want to know how long I was out?" I ask, digging the pen deeper into the paper.

"Two days. It's Monday. Z, what's the point of you having a phone if you don't check it?"

"Two days," I repeat in horror, turning in my chair to face him. I regret it instantly, catching him still shirtless and drawing a studded belt through the loops of his black trousers. *Stupid, wicked brain.* "Shouldn't you be on a tour bus headed to another city?"

Hail slips a black sleeveless shirt over his torso, the muscles in his arms flexing. "Luckily Liam had a guest performance with another band on Saturday. Sunday was a rest day, but we're headed to France this evening. I got you something to eat. Want me to heat it up for you?"

Before I can fully process the fact that he took care of me for two whole days or turn his offer of food down, my stomach growls loud enough for him to hear. He chuckles, then gets to work reheating something in a plastic container from the fridge. He sets the warmed food in front of me.

"Hope you don't mind Mediterranean food. I'd picked up some on Friday but ended up eating it all when you kept sleeping, so I went back and got more last night."

I don't like it. I fucking *love* it. After devouring my portion, Hail offers up another container of chicken and rice.

"I can order more food. I usually have two lunches and dinners." He shrugs, revealing that classic, sweet grin I've come to adore.

So I polish off his half of the food, too, then return to working on the song that was the interlude for my nightmares. Hail sits in a chair opposite of me and picks out a chunky riff on a black seven string guitar. The delicious image elicits a bit of drool along my bottom lip.

Once I feel in control of my brain again, I hold out the lyrics for his review. His gaze meets mine in question. He sets his guitar down and reaches for the notebook. I analyse every little shift in his features while he reads the words he inspired, both with his tenderness and his musical talent.

"This is good, Z." He runs through a few melancholy chords, humming the words. Goosebumps pop up on my arms, and I have the sudden desire to hear him sing for real. Does he do smooth vocals on any tracks for Atonement? I'm sure as hell going to spend some time finding out.

"You cool if I share this with Liam? It's not out to the public, but he's got eyes on a studio back home. He might let us record something. Only if you're comfortable with it, of course."

I smile at him, enticed by the dream of visiting Hail across the ocean but knowing it's a stretch. "I think I can handle that."

Hail's eyes go wide as he blinks back at me. I glance down at his beautiful hands, wondering what they would feel like moving over my body the way they glide over a guitar. Wondering how quickly he would put them on me if I asked.

Carefully, he tears out the page from my notebook and folds it to fit in his back pocket. He stretches a hand out to rest against my forehead. Brows furrowing, my hands shoot up, feeling for the curls of my hair to find that they've been tied up by a little rubber band.

Hail's laugh is low and throaty. "It's cute. You're cute."

My entire face heats as we stay that way for a moment, both of my hands covering his. I swallow and try to remember to breathe.

Hail pulls away and motions to a large plastic bag on the floor beside the bathroom. "I got you a few things. You can shower if you want. Or if you're still hungry, we can order something in. Or we could watch a movie."

Catching the little jittery bounce of his knee, I bite down on my lip at the realisation that he rambles when he's nervous. Holding back another smile, I reply, "I'll shower, thanks."

His fingers brush against my forearm as I pass him. Eyes going wide, I glance down at him still sitting on the bed. Desire rushes through me as I imagine easing him onto his back. Running my tongue along the V of his waist I know is hidden beneath his shirt. Straddling him and capturing his perfect mouth with my own.

His rich whiskey eyes shimmer with emotion. "Whatever you need, Z, I want you to know that I'm here for you."

Sadness swells in my chest when I think about him leaving today. All I can do is nod.

I take a quick shower, not keen on spending too much time in there again. I don't really feel like being cooped up inside either when I've been trapped in the dark for too long.

Lips twitching with a smile, I exit the bathroom dressed in the white Atonement t-shirt and black trousers he gave me. Trousers that fit far too nicely. The guy has a knack for detail and a heart a mile wide.

"You're pretty smooth, you know that," I murmur as his gaze roves over me.

"What can I say?" He cracks a grin. "Never thought I'd be the possessive type, but my band name looks good on you."

Fuck. Boundaries. We need boundaries. It would be so easy to fall into this with him, even though it's a recipe for disaster.

I brush a hand along the back of my neck. "I should probably go home."

Hail's expression crumples, and I feel the weight of his disappointment heavy in my chest. "I, uh, I actually booked this room for you for another day. So don't feel like you need to rush."

"Oh."

How do I navigate this? How can I repay him for his kindness? I could hang around for a bit longer. Write another song or two to share with him, hoping they'll turn into something. Maybe they won't. Maybe I'm avoiding going home.

He rises to his feet. "I'm being inconsiderate. If you want me to leave you alone-"

"I don't," I reply too quickly.

"Okay."

"Okay."

"Hey, do you want to go fuck around town?" I ask, latching on to that bubble of what feels like happiness inside of me.

His smile makes a comeback, spreading warmth through every atrophied part of my body. "Fuck around with you? Hell to the yes."

The notorious vanished singer of the progressive metal band, Visage, tours me around London. Apparently, he was born and raised here, though he doesn't seem enthusiastic about that fact. Or maybe he's not keen on talking about his childhood, and that's what has every visible muscle in his body tensing up.

Selma warned against digging for information, but I can't help my curiosity. I just want to get to know the guy. Is that such a crime? I choose my questions delicately, not wanting to trigger his instinct to flee. I think he'd take a little chip off my heart if he suddenly disappeared.

"Have you traveled much outside of London?" I peek over at him as we stroll along a road nestled beside the Thames river.

He chews on his bottom lip. "Toured Europe quite a bit."

I wait anxiously for him to elaborate, desperate for more pieces of him. What was his demise? What could have stolen away his chance at a future in music? Not that he doesn't still have a chance at it. One leaked nugget of information and he could be on top where he belongs.

When he gives me nothing, I change the topic. "How old are you?"

"Twenty-seven." He meets my gaze, awaiting my reaction. Dear sweet Jesus, he was young when Visage started to take off.

"You?" he asks.

I crack my knuckles against my palm. "Thirty-one. Getting old for a rockstar, right?"

He dips his head to hide a little smile. To my absolute delight, he reaches out and takes my hand. "Come on, rockstar. There's a quiet place ahead where we can grab some dinner."

Squeezing his hand, I follow him under a bridge between the London Eye and the Palace of Westminster. We discover a small food truck parked beneath it. Z retrieves a sad wad of pounds from the jeans I bought him, and I have a thought to offer to pay instead, but I don't want to make him uncomfortable. He hasn't outright told me he's struggling with money, so I shouldn't just assume that's the problem.

I inhale my basket of fish and chips at impressive speed. While he tosses our trash, I jog down the street to buy us tickets for the London Eye. It might be cheesy, but it's something I want to do. Or really, I just want to spend more time with him before the band hops back on the tour bus.

If I had it my way, Z would come with us. The thought strikes me to ask. I mean, if he's considering working with me, and he doesn't have a stable place to live, why shouldn't he ride along?

We climb into one of the spacious viewing pods on the giant ferris wheel contraption. I thank my lucky stars that we get the pod to ourselves. Z sits on the edge of one of the center benches, gaze locked on me as I move to the glass windows and drink in the London cityscape painted on a backdrop of cloudy gray sky.

"Best tour guide ever." I praise him.

His voice is soft and faintly threaded with nerves. "Where are you from?"

"Highland Park, Texas." Smirking, I turn my head to look at him. "Do you know where that is, Z?"

He winces. "I know where Texas is. Hard to miss it."

Pivoting toward him, I'm unable to stop my legs from closing the distance between us. He looks too solemn hunched over on the bench, so I sink between his spread legs. He sucks in an audible breath as he watches my hands slide up his thighs. Slowly, he raises those icy eyes to mine as his hand slips behind my neck. His other hand cradles my face in reverence.

Giving in to need, if only for today, I lean in and fit my mouth to his. Electricity sparks through me as his body melts. I grip his lean waist with both hands, clinging to this moment. To him. To us. To the idea of a future.

Damn it. I'm so done for. This feels right. I've never had eyes for men, at least, that I can remember. Could have been a subconscious thing.

Or maybe Z was just made for me.

His lips and tongue move soft and slow against mine, savoring. It's unlike anything I've experienced.

It's everything.

When he breaks the kiss, his forehead rests against mine. His voice is dipped in pain. "Why am I so captivated by you?"

"I think you've got that backwards, Z. It's you who holds me hostage." I steal another kiss, trying to ignore my straining dick, begging for more. We don't need to give London an exhibition.

My lips hover over his. "Agree to work with me." Another kiss. "You can call our band whatever you want. We can play anything. We can just record in the privacy of our homes. Or we can play a few little venues like you do here when my tour is done. I'm down for anything, as long as it involves you."

His fingers glide into the longer hair at the top of my head, stroking gently against my scalp. I shut my eyes and hum in approval.

"Okay," he whispers.

My eyes snap open, and I try to decipher the emotions warring on his face. Sadness. Panic. Excitement.

"And what if I want you to travel with us?" My heart slams against my ribs, ready to break shit if it doesn't get its way.

His mouth opens, rejection sitting visibly on his trembling bottom lip, so I fight harder. Wrapping a hand around his wrist, I raise it to press a kiss to his palm.

"What's stopping you, Z?"

"So many things," he replies. With a heavy eye roll, his shoulders slump. "The most pertinent being I need a job."

I straighten up. "Liam just fired his guitar tech. We need somebody to step in through the end of the tour. I've seen how well you play. And you already know him. Sort of."

Z brushes locks of hair from his face, tugging on the ends like he's in agony. "I don't want handouts, Hail."

"Liam won't give it to you if you're not a good fit. He's too much of a control freak to let anyone touch his instruments." I scrunch up my nose. "Just promise me you won't fall for his seduction."

This gets a small laugh out of him, and I wrap my arms fully around his waist, burying the side of my face against his rapidly beating heart.

"Only if you promise not to influence his decision."

"Done deal. There's no influencing Liam to do anything. Trust me."

After a few moments of silence, his fingers return to my hair. "This... between us, it's not a good idea."

"I've not been known to make good decisions," I admit with a chuckle. "But I'll accept whatever you're comfortable giving me. Just know that this is new for me, too. You're the first guy I've been into."

The doors to the pod open, signaling the end of the ride. However, I'm not done with him. Easing my hand into his silky dark hair, I admire him properly. Even without his hood and mask, he's still hiding. No fooling me, though. I can see the beauty beneath. The quiet strength. He just needs the right environment to channel it, one where he's lifted up. Encouraged.

I kiss him one more time, relishing in the softness of his pouty mouth. It's the little sigh he lets out that seals my fate.

There's really no coming back from this.

After interviewing with the very intimidating Liam, their band manager, Sondra—a woman I recognise having mothered me a few nights before—and two other techs to see if I can vibe, I sign a short-term contract to tour with Atonement as a guitar tech. Short-term because this is Liam's last tour with the band. I have to sign an NDA about that, too.

Hail wasn't kidding, though. Liam didn't give me any special treatment. He asked difficult questions, spending hours with me on FaceTime while they continued their tour to assure I could handle his tuning and preferences for the stage. I'll have to keep three of his guitars in top shape, polished and restrung. I'll have to help move equipment, too, sometimes early in the morning, almost always late at night.

Not to mention, Liam stares at me as if he's trying to get a deep read of my soul, which makes me itch in my own skin. But if I'm confident in anything, it's playing and caring for instruments. As long as I can maintain focus, I know I won't fuck this up.

Before the ink on my contract even dried, Sondra had me flown out to Atlanta to meet up with the band. France was their last European stop, and now they're on to sweep the United States.

To say I'm nervous about meeting the other members of Atonement is an understatement. I'm petrified. When I played festivals and venues, I rarely socialised with the others. And even if I did, it was always after I'd consumed a fuckton of drugs or alcohol. Sometimes a combination of both.

Exiting the plane, I fire off a text to Hail to let him know I've arrived.

Hurry that cute ass up! Is it wild to admit that I missed you?

A smile plays on my lips. Above his message is his congratulatory selfie on landing the job. I definitely didn't save it to my photo album.

I find him posted up at the curb outside the airport entrance sporting a backwards hat and sunglasses. *What a lame disguise.* His black Bad Omens shirt does little to hide his definition or tattoos. But I don't mind the sight.

Swallowing my nerves, I roll my suitcase up to the ostentatious black SUV he's standing in front of.

"Yay, Liam didn't eat you alive." Immediately, he sweeps me into a hug, a risky move with countless pairs of eyes on us. Still, I find it impossible to pull away from him. Hail feels like home, even though I don't know what that should feel like. This has to be close. His touch temporarily fills that emptiness in my chest, and I hate myself for it.

Focus on work. Focus on work.

When I informed Selma that I'd be touring with Atonement, she told me, with love, not to come back. Told me I better experience everything Mykhail Koval had to offer me or we wouldn't be on speaking terms.

Considering Selma's my only friend, if I can even call her that with my lack of effort, I take that threat seriously.

"You hungry?" Hail asks after we climb into the SUV. Rapidly, he becomes flustered as he forgets where the turn signal is located. The windshield wipers snap back and forth with vigor, and he matches their shrill, dry screeches with cuss words.

"What, was the rental agency all out of fancy cars today?" I tease.

Hail purses his lips in a pout. "Liam threatened to fuck me up if I took the sports car this time. He always gets dibs on the nicer shit."

A gentle laugh escapes me as he starts the vehicle and merges out onto the street. The lanes here are so wide, it's no wonder Americans keep designing bigger vehicles.

"Back to my original question. Food?" Hail glances over at me. In the privacy of the SUV, he lets his eyes peruse freely. I squirm in my seat. I dressed down for the flight, choosing grey joggers and a tattered black hoodie, but he doesn't seem to mind.

"Food," I agree, running a hand over my growling belly.

Hail pulls into a parking lot in front of what looks like somebody's house. It's a brown brick building with a few tables and umbrellas scattered in the paved front yard. The inside is reminiscent of a pub back home, and when we're handed menus, I can't help but sink my teeth into my bottom lip to hold back a hearty laugh.

"This is British food."

Hail fidgets in his chair. "Shit. Do you want to go somewhere else? I panicked over what American food to feed you. Decision-making is hard with ADHD." He flushes and looks at the front door like he wants to escape. "I knew I should have gone with chicken instead."

"This is good." His expression remains like that of a wounded animal, so I add, "Seriously, Hail. You did perfect."

His smile returns, and my heart stumbles. For a moment, I let myself take him in. The life that shines from within him is like staring at the sun without the threat of permanently burning your eyes.

We order pretzels with mustard and cheese to start. The waiting staff offers beers, and Hail orders one, but then changes his mind when I stick with water.

"I didn't even ask if you drink." He frowns.

Nerves prickle under my skin. "I don't."

When he starts messing with his silverware and straightening the salt and pepper shakers, I'm desperate to put him at ease. "It's okay. You can get a beer. It doesn't bother me. I made a choice to quit it after some struggle with addiction years ago."

Some struggle is a stretch, but I downplay it to keep him from worrying more. It's the first real sliver of my darkness I've offered up. We don't need to take a deep dive into my ugly past while trying to enjoy a meal.

Hail nods. "Liam doesn't drink either."

"He came to Selma's bar with you," I comment, swiping another bite of pretzel in the melty cheese. God, I missed savory food. With my new job, I look forward to experiencing American fast food and copious amounts of snacks, but not until I've paid some bills. I should be able to catch up on Mum's house payment with two paychecks. Then I'll start chipping away at her treatment facility balance.

"For some unknown reason, he lets me torture him." Hail shrugs. "Like you, he made a choice at a young age never to touch it after witnessing how it can destroy more than one life."

Swallowing down unpleasant feelings crawling up my throat like insects, I ask, "You've known each other a while, then?"

"Yeah, forever. Though Liam can be pretty antisocial. He comes and goes as he pleases, but he's always there for me when it matters most."

My brother was that for me. No one else has come close to filling that role.

The wait staff brings my chicken beurre blanc and Hail's shepherd's pie. He watches me take a bite, eyes wide in wonder.

My chuckle is low. "Would you like some?"

"It just looks so good. We could, like... split?" He pushes his plate toward me and we end up dividing up our meals.

We chat about our favourite cities to visit, all the little unknown places we discovered. I'm transfixed as he gets into enthusiastic detail about an off-the-grid castle he and the band explored on their first tour of Ireland that sparked inspiration for lyrics to one of their most popular songs.

Then we craft outrageous tales for the people in the restaurant. By some miracle, I make Hail shoot Coke out of his nose when I create a whole CIA backstory for sunglasses guy in a Hawaiian button-up sitting at the bar.

"Jesus, I haven't done that since I was a kid." He wipes at his face, head shaking in disbelief.

Watching him in awe, I realise this is my first outing with a friend. Not a bandmate. Not a schoolmate. Not a fan. There are no expectations. No desire to numb anything, either. It's just me and Hail, and he seems happy to be in my company.

I could be fooling myself, though.

"Thank you for this," I say, cheeks warming.

Hail's smile grows to a blinding wattage. "Fuck, are there hearts in my eyes right now?"

The hot blood from my face floods through the rest of my body, and I have to drop my gaze to our cleaned plates.

After some debate over splitting the bill—he demands to pay since I bought our dinner in London—Hail takes my hand and leads me toward the door, just like he did that day in the cafe. More than a few pairs of eyes trail us, but I keep my focus on the back of his tan neck.

I need to put a stop to this, but the part of my brain that's satisfied to let him lead is in charge today. Work technically doesn't start until tomorrow. I can enjoy myself for one more day.

Out in the evening air, the sun paints the sky in beautiful streaks of fading rose gold and baby blue as it dips below the tree line. Hail walks me to the passenger door, something of a habit it seems. I'm curious to know what else I can come to expect from him.

Hail's nose wrinkles as he fiddles with the car keys. "Fair warning, the other guys in the band can be a bit much. They're extremely friendly. Just... like hyper."

I nod, though I can't help but rub my hand along the back of my neck. Slowly, Hail leans in and presses a gentle kiss to my cheek. My limbs freeze up as my pulse races.

"Sorry," he whispers, but he stays hovering near the corner of my mouth.

I lick my lips, my heart lurching in my chest. I shouldn't give in, but some invisible force pulls me closer to him.

"Don't be," I reply softly. Gripping the ends of my sleeves, I turn my head and meet his lips with my own.

He clams up, and panic unfurls in my chest. *Fuck.* What if he didn't want that out in the open? What if he thought he was interested, but he's had a change of heart? I told myself I would keep things professional. I've lasted all of what, a couple of days?

Hail pushes me against the side of the SUV. I grunt against his mouth in surprise as his hips pin me there. One hand moves to cradle my face as the other drops to my hip. His tongue sweeps along my bottom lip and pries me open. The little groan he unleashes awakens lust in me like I've never known, as we roll our tongues against each other.

He breaks away when we hear car doors shutting nearby, though he rests his forehead against mine. We're both panting. I'm flushed from head to toe and a little dazed.

"Z, I need you to remove yourself from my hands before I take this too far."

I lean in to press my mouth to his cheek, returning his sweet gesture that got us into this position in the first place, before I dip under his arm and break the sexual tension.

Swallowing, I reach for the car door. When I sink into the seat and buckle in, I tell myself that was the last time I'll ever kiss Hail Koval. It has to be, no matter how much my wounded heart wants to shatter all over again at the thought.

Hail drives us to a nearly empty parking lot at a golf course.

"Not exactly the scene I was expecting," I say, though I'm glad to keep a distance from the typical rockstar hangouts.

He chuckles. "Fame doesn't mean we instantly become cool, Z. We're all just a bunch of southern boys who like to do stupid shit in our free time."

I'm thoroughly perplexed by the environment we walk into, greeted by clean-cut employees in polos and khaki shorts in the front shop. They don't seem alerted by our appearances, which means they've been clued in on Atonement's visit. And with the late hour, the usual crowds have dwindled.

"You play?" Hail asks with a smirk, as he holds the back door to the course open for me. Muggy air hits me like a sauna. I breathe straight humidity into my lungs.

"Never," I admit, wrinkling my nose. "Sports weren't my thing."

Not exactly true. My mum just didn't want to spend the money on them. I didn't find a passion for anything until my aunt bought me my first keyboard for Christmas. After that, I helped in her gardens every summer to earn enough allowance for a new instrument. Then I would spend the entire school year obsessively learning how to play it. As soon as my mum recognised my talent, all of a sudden she became interested in paying for music lessons.

Loud bantering draws my attention to a group of guys lurking beside four parked golf buggies. Even if they hadn't been so boisterous, it would have been easy to pick them out among the backdrop of golfers. They look like they're about to pose for a gothic magazine, dressed in mostly black and dripping confidence gained through fame.

"Buzz cut is Griff, our drummer," Hail informs me.

Interesting. Griff seems to be the only one in the group without tattoos and piercings. He's shorter than the rest too, but there's a grace to his movements the others lack.

"Spiky red-head is Malek," Hail continues.

Malek's wearing a visor covered in tiny metal badges and safety pins. He's got the most dangerous smile, like a Venus flytrap, gauges with little snakes running across the hole, and a shag of longish hair styled to almost dagger-like points.

"You've seen Liam. He's my best friend." Hail leans in closer. "And don't worry too much about charming Layla, the woman next to him. She rarely hangs out longer than a quick hook-up with Liam."

I quirk a brow at Layla, dressed in combat boots, a mini-skirt, a camo bra under a sheer black top, and wearing more hooped earrings than I can count. She's currently drinking in Liam like he's the last pool of water in a desert. His body is turned entirely away.

Hail swaggers up to them and gives Liam a bear hug before slapping the other two guys on the sides of their heads. "Guys, this is Z. Liam's new guitar tech."

Hail doesn't mention anything about our collaboration, and I have to wonder if he's told them about it. Maybe we won't be working on anything while I'm the hired help.

I'm not one to judge. I carry secrets of my own.

To my surprise, Griff pulls me into a hug, patting at my back like we're old friends. "Good to meet you, man. Welcome to the fam."

"Sup, dude," Malek greets me with a jerk of his chin. "Sorry, Griff's a toucher."

Waggling his brows, Malek earns a headlock from Griff.

My gaze falls on Liam next. He holds out a hand for me to shake. "Glad you made it to Atlanta in one piece," he says in a smooth baritone.

"Yeah, thanks." Heat coasts over my cheeks. I'll have to get that under control if we're going to be working closely together.

Liam leans in closer. "Interested to see what you two come up with." Then his eyes flick between me and Hail as if he's trying to uncover the hidden connection there. More for protection of Hail, I ease a bit away from Hail's side. Are the others aware of his recent... preferences?

"Let's fucking hit it, boys!" Hail yells out, and we all load into golf buggies, Malek and Griff in their own buggies, tearing off for the first hole. I cling to the roof as Hail guns it after them, still on edge after meeting new people and adapting to a strange environment.

When we make it to the first patch of trimmed grass, Griff's already shot his ball into the pond. He stomps off after it while Malek laughs maniacally. Then, with a perfect swing, Malek drives his ball onto the green.

"Well, fuck me to tears, rich kid. That was a good shot." Hail shouts out, then turns to me. "Malek grew up with a golf course in his neighbourhood."

My brows furrow as we slide out of the buggy, failing to understand how that could be a proper place to live.

"Wouldn't all the houses have broken windows?"

Chuckling, Hail reaches around me to grab a club, his face coming close enough to mine to kick-start my heart.

I can't help my eyes dragging up and down his form as he lines up a shot. His feet do this silly little tippy tap thing before he hammers the ball over the pond, nearly sinking it in the hole.

"Rich kid?" I ask, cocking a brow at him.

"Oil money." He beams. "Can you imagine my dad's face when I told him I didn't want to get a degree in finance?"

I can't help a small smile. "That pleased?"

"Thrilled." He holds out the club for me. "You're up, babe."

God bless my weak heart and the way it's fluttering. I make a quick sweep behind us to assure Liam didn't overhear. I've been out of the closet since I was twelve, but I worry for Hail and what the world might think if it gets leaked that he's taken an interest in me, of all people.

Could be I'm just scared to get found out after five years of crypt silence dwelling in the shadows. But honestly, I can't name more than a handful of metal artists that have publicly come out. I can't be included in that group because no one actually knows who the fuck I am.

Hail gives me a cocky grin. "Scared to lose?"

I drag my hoodie off, reveling in the way his eyes dip to the patch of skin above my boxers before my shirt falls back into place. Then I snatch the club out of his hand, my fingers brushing over his. How can even the simplest touches make me crave more? Though, I won't be the one to pursue. I made a promise to myself not to get involved enough to hurt him. That's the best thing I can do to protect his heart.

"You fucking wish." I smirk, and Hail's eyes shimmer with amusement.

After studying his form, I assumed I had a grasp on what to do. However, my first swing results in an absolute bloody miss that nearly pops my spine out of place. Malek's wild laughter erupts from across the pond.

"Felt the wind on that one," he shouts, bending in half to slap his knee.

"Fuck you, too." I counter, and Griff busts out in laughter this time.

This feels… too comfortable. It reminds me of the simple days with Visage before we got a taste of success and everything fell apart. Is this what it could have been like for us?

I rub guitar-calloused fingers between my brows. *Don't go there.*

My second swing is a success. The ball barely clears the pond, but hell, that's a win in my book.

By the time we play through eight holes, I've drained my bottle of water. A lady the others have titled Queen Callie drives by with a drink buggy and passes out another round of beers and waters, beaming at the attention Malek and Griff are bestowing upon her.

"Sloppy drunks." Hail shakes his head.

Tuning into the current of excitement, I jump into the driver's seat before Hail can make it back to the buggy. He's all smile as he slips in next to me. "Where you taking me, sunshine?"

I press the pedal to the floor, cutting Malek and Griff off before a narrow bridge over the pond. Hail fails to sip at his beer as the buggy bounces over planks, and I chuckle when he lifts a middle finger out of the buggy like a flag of victory.

Stealing a look at his profile, I want to soak in the absolute passion for life he radiates. There's something to be said about surrounding yourself with the type of people you want to become. He's a fucking gem, and I can only hope this bubbling emotion inside of me lasts forever.

He catches me staring. "Do I need to drive so you don't crash this thing, Z?"

I grin. "You have freckles on your cheeks."

Brows furrowing, he works his bottom lip between his teeth. "Do not."

"You do. I like them."

We reach hole nine. Liam seems satisfied to hang back and take his time, though his partner's more interested in playing on her phone than participating. Malek blasts Atonement's new album from his phone, earning questioning looks from the few golfers left out on the course at the late hour.

God, this night has done wonders to liberate me. We're tearing shit up, bounding over hills and down valleys, whacking the crap out of a tiny white ball like we don't have a care in the world.

I park at the next tee box. There's a bit of a gap between us all now, Griff and Malek in a race to finish first, and Liam still highly concerned about performing at his best. He's such a conundrum, both carrying an air of not giving a shit while also putting his all into his current task.

"You bored yet, Z?" Hail rests a hand on my thigh, and I shift on the seat as my dick twitches.

"Not at all," I reply, unable to tear my eyes away from where he's touching me. "I get why this sort of thing can be... fun."

Only because I'm here with them. Only because they're showing me what a real family looks like. Add in the warm evening breeze swaying the lush trees, and

I feel like I've found new purpose. I have no power to shut down this happiness tonight. Even though I know it's short-lived. It's *always* short-lived.

"Do you all do this kind of stuff often?" I ask, as I work my curls up into a tight knot to keep them off my sweaty forehead and out of my eyes. Hail's lips part as he stares at me. He blinks and shakes his head in disbelief. Over what, I have no idea. The fact that my hair can be tamed?

"I wish. It's rare that we all get to take a break. Me and Liam especially, with our dedication to perfection." He stretches his legs out over the front of the buggy. "Tonight's a special occasion. It's Liam's birthday. We thought we'd celebrate by forcing him to play the sport he hates the most."

My brows shoot up. I glance back at Liam, putting on the previous hole. He doesn't look the least bit frustrated. In fact, he's hyper-focused, his ringed and inked fingers gripping the putter. As soon as the ball drops in the hole, he gives the putter a couple of taps on the green. No sign of emotion on his face. A master of control.

Hail snorts on a laugh. "That's his happy dance."

My own laughter fills the air. It's a rare sound, almost shocking me that something so light could be produced from my tainted body.

I could get used to this. The words stick in my throat. I bottle them inside, doubling down on the seal to keep them in place.

Hail's amber eyes dance with mirth. "You ever think about after the music?"

The question hangs in the air. Needing to put my body into motion as I form an answer, I climb out of the buggy and grab the biggest iron just for shits and giggles. Malek twerking next to my target green in taunt has me praying for good aim.

"There's nothing for me after the music," I say quietly, then I line up my shot and smack the ball right over Griff's head, dropping it next to Malek's leather shoes.

"Hit the deck!" Griff shrieks, dropping onto the grass. "Fuckers are trying to kill us!"

Malek leaps onto Griff's back. A wrestling match ensues right in the middle of the course. If they weren't famous, we would have been kicked out hours ago.

From the buggy, Hail cocks his head. "You gonna write songs forever, Z?"

I lick my lips, my heart sinking into my stomach. I don't want to admit to him that I hadn't thought that far ahead. Future wasn't a word that existed in my vocabulary after I let my brother drown. But that's not the kind of thing you dump on someone in the middle of a game of golf.

So I shrug instead. "Maybe. You?"

That masochistic part of me wants to know if I could fit into his vision of a future. Or at least for as long as this gig permits.

"I don't see giving up on music either, but I'd like to give the softer stuff a go for a while. And when I'm too old to get on stage, I'd like to teach lessons."

My chest tightens, and the empty ache there seems more noticeable than before.

"I want a house, too. Low-maintenance, with a giant grill and a pool." Hail sighs, stretching his arms behind his head. "I want to entertain these hooligans. Watch sports and rock out in the garage. All the shit I didn't get to do as a kid since I was forced into activities I didn't give a rat's ass about. Every summer, no lie, I would look forward to practicing music, and I'd get sent off to camps instead. Like my parents couldn't stand to have me breathe the same air as them for more than a weekend."

I drop my head, not wanting to give him an opening to dig into my past. There's not much to tell, anyway.

Reaching for another bottle of water, I down the contents as Hail's gaze bores into me, prodding for that little crack in my armor. I know I'm not being fair, but I'm also trying to keep myself together for the night.

When Hail finally glances away, he lets out a whistle. "Jesus. Someone arrest them."

I turn in time to see Malek ram his golf buggy into the back of Griff's at the peak of a hill. Both of them tip over. Mad laughter ensues from Malek as they tumble out of the buggies.

"I'm not paying for any more damages you assholes leave in your wake!" Liam bellows, his tone shooting my balls up inside my body to hide.

"Liam have any kids?" I ask, cocking a brow.

Hail chuckles. "With the dad tone he's mastered? He really should. He's the oldest of us. Closest to settling down, too."

My head shakes in wonder. It's wild how different people can be from the image the world paints of them. Fans see rock gods. A singer filled with rage. A guitarist with a callous exterior. A bassist and drummer with demonic energy. Fans assume they *know* them. What they like. How they think.

But they don't really know a thing, do they?

By hole eighteen, nearly three hours later, Malek has fallen deep into wild conversation.

"Hey, Griff. What if I just did that? What if I just, like, threw up everywhere? All over the golf course? How long do you think it would take them to clean that up? Or would they just let the sprinklers wash it away?"

Griff tilts his head and runs a hand over his buzzed hair. "Is this another manic thing where you're going to continue to bombard me with hypothetical situations that are so outrageous I won't know how to answer?"

"Yes." Malek nods frantically. "That is exactly what this is."

Griff cracks a wild grin. "Perfect. Let me grab another beer from our first blessed Queen Callie, and I'll entertain your fucked up brain for a while."

I can't help but give a low chuckle. These two are unlike anyone I've met.

"Told you they're a lot," Hail mutters at my side. "We tolerate them only because if we dropped them, I'm certain they would end up outside our bedroom windows with baseball bats. Run away and I'll find you vibes for sure. And maybe they have talent or something."

Liam reaches the tee box and snorts. "Malek broke into my house once because he was out of milk."

Snapping around, Malek points his club at Liam. "Hey, what was I supposed to do? Captain Crunch with crunch berries is worth a police call."

"Normal people go to the store, Malek," Liam grumbles back. "Police should be the last of your worries. You're lucky I didn't break your neck."

We finish up the last hole without injury. Liam's the only one that kept track of his score. I smile as I catch him pocketing the scorecard as memorabilia. Then he slings his arm over Layla's shoulders, cutting for the parking lot where the tour bus has just parked.

Crew members slide into the rental cars, and I follow Hail awkwardly onto their bus, soon to discover that my bag's already been moved to the top bunk in the back.

"Shouldn't I be on a different bus?" I ask, scratching at the back of my neck. "Like for the crew?"

"Nah, this is good." Hail gives me a devious smile.

I try to take up as little space on the couch as possible, but Hail plops down right next to me. His head finds a resting place on my shoulder, and I tense up. He may think he feels a certain way about me, but being bi-curious doesn't necessarily mean he wants to claim a relationship with me in front of his bandmates.

His soft snores come surprisingly fast. I don't have the heart to move him from where he's leaned up against me. Griff and Malek are too engaged in a video game to take notice, and Liam's in the back bedroom with his female friend.

I stay awake through most of the drive to Nashville, fighting off the rising guilt of this normalcy and how nice it feels to belong somewhere, even if it's temporary.

Drifting in and out of focus as the bus hums along the pitch-black open highway, I look down at Hail's head in my lap. My heart stutters as I study him and wonder how lucky I am that I got to meet him.

God, there has to be a timeline to this. I cannot fuck up his life, too.

I let my fingers trace over his straight brows and long lashes. Then I map the curve of his mouth and the strong line of his square jaw and the shell of his ear, broken up by piercings.

My hand drops from his face when Liam materialises from the back of the bus, shirtless and wearing black cargo trousers that hug his powerful thighs. He's absolutely ripped, his body belonging to someone better suited to the ring than the stage.

Though my heart is racing, Liam doesn't even blink twice at us as he strides over to the fridge and tugs it open. "Need something?"

"Uh…" I lick my lips nervously. "Water would be great. Thanks."

He holds a bottle out for me, then cracks his own bottle open and downs it in one go. He dips his head to each side, releasing audible pops. "Fuck. I'm tired of touring."

I stare up at him in awe. Okay, so maybe not MMA bound. He has a presence that belongs on screen. It's not a thing that can be faked. He had to have been born with this strong, silent confidence.

Liam leans against the counter, his gaze falling on Hail. "I'm glad he's found someone that makes him smile."

Risking judgment, I twirl a lock of Hail's golden hair around a finger. "Is he not usually this happy?"

Liam tilts his head, long hair spilling down his torso. "It's rare to see him down, but I know he's struggling with my decision to leave the band. Add that to his loneliness since his family made him feel less for his life choices and his last relationship ending badly."

I find it hard to swallow. "What would they think… about…"

Us. I let the question fade. It's something I shouldn't ask. There is no us. There will never be an us. Still, I want to know, for Hail's sake. For his future, when he finds his soulmate.

Liam scratches at his chin. "It would be the equivalent of tossing an angry beehive inside the window of an occupied house. Lots of screaming and cussing."

"Ah." I swallow, grimacing. "Do they keep in touch?"

"He talks with his twin sister every now and then to check in, but she's pretty busy with her DPT program and internship."

I try to imagine Hail with a sister, and it's easy to visualise the two of them, probably both fair-haired and tan, arms slung over each other and sporting broad smiles.

"Yeah, she's got that same fucking beautiful soul, too," Liam mumbles. Then he sighs, his head turning toward the back of the bus as sadness reflects in his dark eyes.

My brows knead together. "You're very protective of him."

A question, though I've only seen Liam with women, and I know for a fact Hail's dipping his feet into unknown waters with me.

"He's been the only person in my life I can trust," Liam answers, his gaze meeting mine with enough intensity to liquify my bones. "When you witness darkness, you tend to be lured to the light. He is my light."

I nod, picking up on the underlying meaning of his words. His warning.

Focus on work. Focus on work.

Liam pushes off the counter and tosses his empty water bottle away. "You need help getting him in his bunk?"

My head lowers to Hail. "I think I'll stay like this for a while longer."

Without another word, Liam vanishes, leaving me with very mottled feelings about our conversation, mostly because now I'm even more worried about corrupting the soul that Liam guards so fiercely.

FOURTEEN

Hail

He's all mine.

This thought shoots a thrill through my veins until I'm nearly buzzing, as Z and I find ourselves alone on the tour bus for the first time in days.

He's put in long afternoons and evenings trailing the backline crew and religiously studying Liam's playing. Guitars are always polished to a blinding shine and restrung with care. But that's not surprising. Z's toured before, enough to know to keep an *oh shit* cable on stat.

Liam murmured praise to him last night after our show, and I swear I saw Z stand an inch taller.

The time apart has allowed me space to sift through my feelings as I try to figure out what's happening between us. I want to make sure I'm not just experimenting with him. I don't want to hurt him.

But I keep coming back to a place of raw need when I see a text from him or glimpse him running around backstage or giving me shy smiles from the sidelines during our performances.

God, don't get me started on what he does to my pulse when I see him sporting band merch. His Atonement beanie over those wild, dark locks? Yeah, I'm into that.

I need his company. I need his kisses. I think I need more, and I haven't felt that way since my ex took a sledgehammer to my heart.

I never thought I would consider something serious with someone again after that relationship went up in hellfire. All the effort I pumped into that woman. All the money spent on combining our lives only to find out she'd been sharing it *and* our bed with her boss.

Dropping onto the couch next to Z as he crouches over his notebook, scribbling away, I soak in his profile. I don't have the right words to describe what he does to me internally, only that I feel buoyant. Weightless. Content.

"Is this part of the contract? Getting to watch me work?" Z murmurs, dipping his chin. His hair lifts up slightly to reveal the smooth column of his neck. Blood rushing low in my body, I can't help but lean over and press my mouth to it. I linger there, running the tip of my nose across his skin. He smells like clean soap with a hint of vanilla.

I groan. It's not enough. I want to taste him. Taking his notebook from his hand, I toss it onto the table across the bus.

"That's not going—"

With one hand, I turn his head to capture his mouth with my own. Oh god, yeah, I like this too much. It takes a few quick heartbeats before Z's kissing me back. He sinks into my touch. I shift our bodies until we're half laid out on the couch, me between his parted legs. My hips pressing against him. My dick straining for more as I rock my hips and stroke my tongue against his.

"Is this too much?" I rasp, dragging my lips down his jaw and back to his neck.

The door to the bus opens, and I rip myself from his body. Z straightens up and rakes his fingers through his messy hair. His lips are red from me punishing them, and there's a clear hickey near his collar. I reach out to adjust his shirt higher as Malek and Griff climb on.

"Yeah, but, like... if an alien took you, they would just zap your mind to forget. We could all be walking around with implants or some shit and not even know it," Malek carries on, oblivious to what was just occurring. Thank god we had the curtains over the windows drawn or we might have made a very public display of my newest obsession.

"Let's file away alien talk for when I'm drunk, alright?" Griff answers. He turns to us, and I lift a hand, trying to hide my irritation at having been interrupted. How far would I have taken things if we'd been left alone longer?

"What's good, boys?" Griff calls out, opening the fridge to grab a beer. He drops onto the couch next to me and grabs the remote. "You all just sitting in the dark?"

"Uh, no." I swallow and drag my fingers through the longer portion of my hair. "We were working on some music. I guess I didn't realize how late it had gotten."

I peek over at Z, who looks down at his hands clenched in his lap.

Why couldn't Malek and Griff have stayed out longer? Should Z and I sneak into the back? Would that be too obvious?

There's apprehension in Z's face, especially when his gaze drifts to the back of the bus like he's ready to hide. As much as I want him to do as he pleases, I also really want his company. I want him to be in our company, too. I want more of his smiles. His laughter. His happiness.

My fingers stealthily brush against the back of his neck, sliding into his hair. Is it wrong of me to plead with my gaze? To make demands of him when I've already injected myself into his life?

Settling deeper into the couch, Z finally asks, "What are we watching?"

Griff cracks a smile. "Buckle up. Tuesdays are for horror, my good sir."

We arrive in Kentucky early enough to fuck around on set for a while. These are some of my favorite moments. An empty venue. No screaming fans. No pressure or structure. Just pure music streaming out in its rawest form during soundcheck.

I motion for Z, tinted in blue light on the side of the stage. He shakes his head, pointing to Liam. *Working*, he mouths back.

I envy his dedication. I really do.

"Liam, tell Z to get his ass out here," I demand.

Liam doesn't miss a beat. "Guitar! Now!" he orders Z.

Alright, so maybe I do have some influence over Liam, but Z earned his position with the crew. I didn't meddle; I swear on my life.

Z rushes over, holding out Liam's black Les Paul. Liam takes it from his hands, only to drape it over Z's shoulders. My chest swells with pride at my chosen brother being acceptant of the guy I like. That's a toasty fucking feeling right there.

Liam and I had a conversation about my obvious crush last night. He wasn't judgmental. Just cautious out of his love for me. He warned me that I can't fix Z. Can't make him want to piece himself back together. Only Z understands the pattern of his wounded mind.

After a moment of hesitation, Z settles into the instrument, his fingers warming up over the strings. Satisfaction rushes through me. *This* is where he belongs. Not backstage. I know it in my bones. But for some reason, he backed away from it all. Human nature makes me curious to dig into that mystery. Respect for Z and the desire for his trust keep me from Googling and asking prying questions.

Z drifts under the spotlights at the front of the stage as they shift to a haunting red, looking like my wet fucking dream with his dark hair and perfect, angelic features. If any of my bandmates were watching close enough, they would catch me drooling.

Jesus fuck, fans would not have been able to handle him unmasked. With how feral everyone was over his hidden identity, he would have never had a moment of peace if they knew what he actually looked like, similar to Tim Henson in the looks and skill department.

Shit, if I hadn't been so consumed with Atonement at that time, I might have jumped on that fan-wagon too.

We're deep into the vibe of an endless, shifting jam, our sound reverberating through the old brick walls of the soaring hall. Some of the crew stop to admire us in between unraveling cords and shuffling boxes of equipment around.

And before I know what the fuck is happening, Z is singing. His deep voice echoes through the expansive space. Griff drops a stick, and I stumble over a chord on my seven string. Goosebumps spring up from head to toe.

It's shocking the way he can drench his words with so much raw emotion, holding out admirable, lengthy notes. He could sing about the weather, and I still think he could move a stadium to tears. It's no wonder Visage was on the verge of something revolutionary.

I am fucking lost. The raw talent of this man... it is on another level. Glancing over at Liam, he nods in agreement at the magic unfolding. I pray he can't see through to just how far I've fallen for Z, but he's known me since we were eight, for fuck's sake.

We play for hours, sweat dripping from our bodies under the warm spotlights. Malek lets out a whoop when we finally cut off. "Leave some for tonight, boys!"

Then he and Griff hurry off in search of cold beer and BBQ. Liam's fingers fly over his phone's keyboard, and then he's gone, too. Afternoon booty call, no doubt.

My gaze wanders to Z, my pulse thundering under too hot skin. He's staring back with wide, panicked eyes, adrift in a sea he doesn't know how to navigate without something to tether him.

I give him a smile and openly check him out. If I wasn't afraid of scarring the crew for life, I'd take him right fucking here.

Damn it, I can't help myself. This thing between us is probably a ticking bomb set to blow me apart from the inside out, but I don't care. A guarded heart can never learn to love again, right?

Handing my guitar to my tech, Cora, and giving her a thumbs up for stellar effort, I stride over to Z. I take care to unstrap Liam's guitar and return it to its case.

I give Z a nod to follow me. Desire reflects in his bright eyes when I flash him a sly grin. He glances around nervously, but everyone's scattering for a break between soundcheck and the show.

He trails after me—my obedient, beautiful addiction. Reaching behind me as I search for a place to hide, I slide my fingers into his. I lead him down a back hall until we find a dark, empty supply room stacked with chairs, dollies, and old stage equipment.

I tug Z inside and shut the door, flicking the lock. A wicked smile graces my mouth as I push him against it. Z looks torn, so I leash myself and wait for a signal from him.

Your move, Z. Show me you want this.

His breathing grows erratic as his eyes drift slowly to my mouth. He licks his lips, and then his mouth collides with mine. His hands grip the front of my shirt, tugging me closer, both of us desperate to taste each other.

It feels like a century since I've been able to touch him like this, unrestrained. Mornings I haven't been able to shake Griff and Malek, and afternoons Z hasn't been keen on taking a break longer than grabbing a bite to eat, solely consumed with learning his job.

I get it. I do. But I'd be lying if I said I wasn't disappointed that I don't get more of his attention.

Pressing my hips against him, I want him to feel every inch of my hard dick. A groan escapes me when his own erection answers.

"Fuck, Z," I utter, one hand delving into his hair and giving it a little tug to draw his head back, giving me better access to his neck. Soon, he's panting and writhing beneath me as I work my tongue up his smooth, warm, salt-tinged skin.

Greedy for him, I run a hand down his chest and lean stomach. I brush my knuckles along his solid length through his jeans. Sparks of pleasure fire along all of my nerves. I grip him tightly, and I'm rewarded with a moan.

I kiss the corner of his mouth, one hand still on his dick and the other wrapped around his jaw. "You like that?"

"Yes." The word comes out more as a hiss.

My fingers swipe below the waistband of his pants, brushing over his silky, warm skin. "Can I touch you, Z?"

"Please," he begs.

"Thank god." I exhale as my hand slips between his pants and boxers to start. "Oh, goddamn. What are you hiding in here?" I nearly dissolve at his rigid size. Could I fit him in my mouth? Could I fit him... elsewhere? Is that something I want?

The visuals playing out in my head pump liquid hot lust to the base of my spine, ruling that a hell yes. I want to fuck him, but I think I'm down to get fucked by him, too.

Z pushes into my hand.

"More?" I ask, nipping at the lobe of his ear.

"Yes," he whispers, shuddering beneath me. I draw my hand out, only to wet my palm with my tongue. He watches in awe, doe-eyed and lips parted. My hand dives inside of his boxers and gives him a few slick pumps from solid base to tip while I claim his mouth.

Unraveling this man is the hottest thing I've ever done. I'm riding the high of adrenaline and desire. And when his hips begin to jerk uncontrollably, matching his frantic breaths, I know he's close to blowing his load.

My brain short-wires on what to do. I've never sucked dick before. Pretty sure you have to prep to take it up the ass, too. Here I got him all worked up for nothing as I fucking fumble with where to take this.

Warm cum seeps down my fingers wrapped around him before I can decide what to do. I'm about to apologize when Z lets out a ragged moan that embeds itself in my very soul.

"Fuckkk." I growl, resting my head on his shoulder. "I'm so fucking into this."

Something inside of Z snaps. He spins us around until I'm the one shoved against the door. With nimble fingers, he flicks open the button on my pants and drags them down, tugging my boxers along with them.

Dropping to his knees, he turns those stunning blue eyes up at me. Does he want me to plead? Because I'm not above it at this point.

"Suck me off," I plead, fisting my cock with the hand still coated in his warm, sticky release. He removes it, replacing it with his own hand, unconcerned about the mess we're making. Then he's taking me into his hot mouth, working me over with devastatingly slow movements. He teases with suction and broad swipes of his tongue and light drags of his teeth on the underside of my crown.

My head drops back against the door as my hips fight to take control and pump into him with reckless abandonment. I've never received such good head in my life. Z sucks dick like he loves the taste. Like he can't get enough of it.

He cups my balls, one of his fingers brushing dangerously close to my hole. I shiver and groan, nearly at the edge. Anything he asked of me, I'd give willingly. He wants to shoot his cum down my throat next time? Done deal. I won't hesitate again.

Z pops off my dick to stroke a finger over my ass. "This okay?"

I don't even hesitate to bark out a yes. His mouth swallows me up again, and his finger swirls over my puckered muscle, slick from the transfer of his cum. The thought of him pushing that inside of me has my thighs quivering and a vein in my foot fucking throbbing with its own heartbeat.

My hand dives into his hair as my eyes lock on the visceral image of him sliding his mouth over my cock.

I explode with a growl, and he sucks up every drop of my release. My muscles and bones go slack, at a loss on how to function properly.

"That was…" I shake my head, still floating down from my cataclysmic orgasm.

Z rises to his feet, his expression a bit lost. I reach for him to anchor him against my chest.

"Are you okay? I didn't mean to lose control like that," he says.

I huff out a laugh. "Z, I jumped your bones, and you're apologizing to me for the best sex of my life? I didn't even fucking reciprocate."

"You did," he murmurs.

"I will. Soon. I want to." I hold him for a few heartbeats. "Let's head back to the hotel and change. Although, I should probably wash the cum off my hand first."

FIFTEEN

Z

I'm a piece of shit for avoiding him.

But what we did in that venue in Kentucky, what I allowed myself to do to him, it can never happen again. Agony spears into me every time I catch Hail's hopeful eyes glancing my way on stage or on the tour bus.

I throw myself further into work and pray that something is being mended inside of me. This new medication seems to be working. The crew doesn't mind my silent company amidst multiple strong personalities. Liam and I have found a good rhythm together. He's mentioned that he's pleased with my work ethic. I even picked out a new guitar pedal for him. He's been using it on stage during performances to get a richer sound.

Even with my honed attention on work, in the quiet moments lying in bed at night, I allow myself to hope. I hope that one day I can be a good enough man for Hail. But I don't have the confidence in myself that I'll ever become one. And I don't have the heart to ask him to wait for me to become what he needs.

Because Hail needs love. Not the darkness I would bring to a relationship. The last thing I want to do is ruin him. There are so many other pure souls out in this world that would give him what he deserves.

So I've become skilled at keeping our conversations to a bare minimum, circling back around to work or picking up an instrument to initiate another jam session with the band on the bus ride between cities.

Eventually, Hail and I will get back to a point where we can collaborate without wanting to jump each other's bones, right?

I can tell it's driving him mad to not get more time with me, but he hasn't outwardly spoken about Kentucky either. Maybe he can sense I need a bit of space. Or maybe he's not as interested as I assumed. Maybe he's mad over what we did. Maybe he decided guys aren't for him. I wouldn't know because I'm too cowardly to use my words to talk to him about any of it.

During our next afternoon break, I sneak off to the tour bus to work on some songs alone. Strumming out a few chords on my acoustic guitar, I lower my head and fall into a melody, eager to purge the sin from my bones.

Spiraling into this hole, death taunts me
Lures me in with the promise of release
From these infinite visions of you broken
My fingers bled trying to fit you back together
Tell me, where is the root of all your pain?
Tell me, how do I begin again?

My head snaps up in horror as Hail appears on the bus. He's panting hard, like he sprinted here all the way from the main festival stage. Was he looking for me?

I'm not worth your effort, I want to tell him. I voice it through my solemn gaze.

I suppose I can't avoid a conversation with him forever. I move to lift my guitar off my lap, but he stops me.

"No, keep playing that song. Please."

"It's not finished—"

"Play, Z. Pretend I'm not here."

He drops into the chair opposite me and rests his elbow on his knees. I let my gaze peruse over him quickly, my heart aching to reach out and touch him. Hold him. Comfort him.

Should I apologise? Or would that land us right back in each other's arms again? Some desperate little piece of me wants that so badly that my hands begin to tremble.

"It's just a rough draft," I whisper.

Hail's expression is fierce. "I don't care. I love to hear you play."

Swallowing, I close my eyes and let my voice caress him as I dive back into that well of pain, desperate to heal internal wounds.

Why can't I get better? Because I don't deserve to. Why do I exist? Because I need to suffer. Why did I agree to this contract? Because I owe a debt.

A stupid tear leaks out of my eye, and Hail's there to sweep it up.

"Z," he murmurs, brows scrunching up. "About what happened in Kentucky. I want you to know, we can take this as slow as you need. If I crossed a line, I'm sorry. But I *am* interested in you. More than I can wrap my head around."

My jaw clenches as I find my body leaning into his touch without instruction. Affection and I aren't well acquainted, so it's no wonder I crave it from him. A fucked up childhood will do that to you.

The bus door squeaks open, and Hail snaps his hand away. He falls back in his chair with a growl of frustration. "I thought you all were headed out for pizza."

Malek glances between us, then his gaze comes to rest on my splotchy face. *Fuck my pale skin.* Can't hide anything.

"Oh, shit. This right here is a mood." Malek plops down on the couch beside me. Griff rubs a hand over his head, taking a seat next to Hail at the table. Liam files in next. He leans against the kitchen counter, arms crossed.

"You homesick, Z?" Liam asks.

"Oh, um... no, I just had something in my eye." I rub it in show, though I catch the way Liam looks at Hail with a sharp gaze.

"Probably dirt. This whole state is a fucking wasteland," Malek says dramatically. He reaches for his bass guitar, rested up against the couch, and begins plucking out some funky notes.

The pain in my chest expands until I'm certain I'll break down in front of all of them. Nothing would be more embarrassing. Sucking in deep breaths, I work to reinforce the locks on my battered emotions.

These guys have been nothing but accepting and kind to me. I don't want to give them a reason to worry or question our developing friendships.

Griff slides his drumsticks out of his back pocket to fiddle with them. "You know, we've all been wondering–"

More exchanged glances between the other three as Hail's eyes burn into the side of my face. He looks like he's ready to leap into action.

"Have you played in a band before, Z?" Griff asks.

Blood drains from my face, panic bleeding darkness into my vision. My head feels too heavy for my neck. Do they know? How did they find out?

I look at Hail, but he gives nothing away in his features.

"I have," I reply carefully. "Feels like a lifetime ago."

"Anyone we know?" Malek asks.

The burning interest of the entire band on me makes me flush and rub the back of my neck. I fight the urge to burst off the bus and sprint somewhere where my brain will feel safe and my chest won't fucking hurt so much. But pulling out of tough situations like this isn't going to help me get over this monster digging its claws into me.

"Probably not," I mutter.

Liar. But I'm not ready to share. I've been doing good. No need to push myself.

"Hard to break into the scene," Malek replies. "I was in three other bands before Atonement took pity on me."

I nod, though I can no longer meet their eyes. Shame burns in my gut. Can we be done with this conversation?

"As you know from the NDA you had to sign, my time is up at the end of this tour. But for the others," Liam waves a hand, "they need a strong guitarist. I've never seen anyone play as well as you. Your name has even been tossed around by Sondra and Cora."

My stomach plummets. All warnings in my brain are firing. Initiate meltdown. I push my fingers harder onto the strings of my guitar. "I'm... not sure that I'd be a good fit."

Hail nudges his shoe against mine. "Don't let it stress you out. If you're not ready, don't worry. We've got time to figure it out."

Time. Isn't that what I want? Could I piece myself together by the end of this tour and find a home with Atonement? Would I want that?

It doesn't matter what I want.

Thankfully, Hail seems to pick up on my approaching limit and changes the subject. "How about that pizza? I'll buy."

Sarcasm ensues, Malek and Griff dramatically bowing in his presence for his contributions. "Thank you, Sir. We are indebted to you for reaching into your coffers to bless us with shit pizza."

Hail shoves at Malek's head, failing to hold back a giggle. "Shut the hell up."

After he calls in an order for the entire crew, Liam offers to pick it up in his new De Tomaso Pantera, purchased and delivered to our hotel last night. Perks of being on his final tour, he's starting to dabble with long-term decisions.

Griff and Malek drift to the back of the bus, fighting over who gets to rinse off first. Hail takes advantage of our moment of privacy, brushing a finger down the shell of my ear. I tilt my head up at him in awe. He is the brilliant sun, and I am a withered plant in desperate need of light.

"You're beautiful," I whisper with a little shake of my head. "But Hail, I am *broken.*"

His jaw clenches. He leans down to press a kiss to my quivering bottom lip, capturing it so perfectly between his. "Then I'll help put you back together."

I don't have the energy to argue with him right now, so I let him snuggle up to me on the couch. He leaves his thigh pressed against mine when Malek wanders back out, dressed in a mesh tank top and black Tripp trousers.

"Halo time?" Malek asks, dropping half onto my lap.

It's become a bit of a guilty pleasure during the long drives. Malek and I even started a campaign. The first moment we got hit with the flood? God, I've never jumped up on a couch that fast in my life. I haven't felt that human in a very long time.

Hail groans. "We can't just chill, can we?"

"Come on, man," Malek complains. "We haven't hung out in ages."

"We were just on stage together! We've been on tour together for what, like, eight years now?"

"That's different and you know it," Malek whines.

Hail rolls his eyes. "How so?"

"Cause on stage we have to share you with everyone," Griff adds in, appearing with a controller already in hand. Malek hands a spare controller to me. He's far too close, but I've learned that this is just how Malek is. Overly affectionate. Goofy. Loyal to a fucking T. And smarter than he leads on with his wild, off-the-cuff chatter.

"Hey, Z." Malek beams. His face is far too close to mine. I can see the different shades of blue and grey in his irises.

"Um, hey," I mumble.

"You're like... really pretty."

"Stop complimenting him," Hail grumbles beside us, suddenly irked.

"I can appreciate, even if I'm straight," Malek replies.

"No. You can't." Hail snaps back. "Not if it makes him uncomfortable."

"Or if it makes *you* uncomfortable," Malek prods, cracking a toothy smile.

My lips quirk. I get the sense that the others have noticed just how close Hail and I can be, but if they've detected anything, they haven't spoken up about it. At least not to me.

"Thank you for the compliment, Malek. Now can you get off my balls, please?" I request, and I catch Hail glaring at Malek's thighs draped over mine. He gives them a shove, and Malek breaks out in giggles.

"When did you become so easy to tease, Hailstorm?" Malek waggles his brows.

I scoot closer to Hail, mostly because I want to assure him that he's my top pick, and partly to give Malek room on the small couch. Hail's arm comes to rest behind my head, his fingers swiping under my hair to draw shivers down my neck. I find myself wanting him to pull me closer. I want to bury my head in his neck. Nip at his ear. Suck a hickey onto his skin. Make him moan my name.

Those illegal thoughts are interrupted by the buzz of Hail's cell in his pocket. He fishes it out, still scowling. After some mumbling on the other line, Hail addresses all of us. "Hey, Liam's hitting the store on the way back. What do you fuckers want for movie night after the show?" He looks at me first, eyes softening.

"Anything sour is good."

His features twist. "Oh no. Z, this arrangement isn't going to work. How can you eat that stuff?"

My brows shoot up. "What? Sour sweets?"

"Yeah." He fakes a look of disgust. "Fucking makes my teeth hurt thinking about it."

"Tell Liam to buy me all the airheads they have," Malek adds.

"Two-liter of Mountain Dew. I don't want to sleep tonight!" Griff whoops, clicking into the menu to start up the game.

I settle in, though there's a looming sense of dread in my gut, knowing I'm allowing them to thread themselves into my very being. If I brace for the pain now, maybe it won't destroy me when I have to rip those stitches out at the end of this tour.

We're in Kansas City and I'm on fucking fire.

I have the fans on strings, and I am the puppet king, drawing them this way and that. Forcing them into aggressive dance. Driving them into madness as we finish our last song and bow.

Stepping up to the mic one last time, I shout out, "Much love, Kansas City! Can I snap a pic?"

It's something I've started doing for my own selfish reason. I want to document Liam's final tour. I want every last piece of this incredible dream we built from the ground up. From senior dropouts to the top of the metal charts. From unwanted teenagers to wanted by millions of fans.

Cheers echo through the venue, loud enough to have me chuckling and shaking my head. "Is that a no, then?"

I love turning the dial up on the noise level, pushing these fans to the limit. They pay good money to escape the mundane. I like to make sure they get our best.

Malek and Griff deserve that, too. If I do decide to call it quits in the metal scene, I want to make sure their careers skyrocket even further. So high that nothing could topple them back to the ground.

Surprisingly, it's Z that rushes my phone out. We lock eyes for too long, both of us panting from physical exhaustion as our hands brush.

Then he's gone, and I feel a creeping sadness as Atonement lines up with our backs to the crowd.

Seeing our grins against a backdrop of fans has guilt striking me in the chest. Is it right for me to think about giving all of this up?

Though, it has been eight long years of this. Constant travel, eating out, late nights and early mornings, catching sickness and pushing myself through it to perform, and yeah, I'll admit a few hangovers in the beginning when we were young and stupid.

Add in the years before we formed Atonement when Liam and I struggled to find loyal bandmates free of addiction, and I've spent almost half my life fighting for this dream. I was okay with the chaos most of the time because I didn't have much else occupying space in my life. But that's how Lizbeth justified cheating. And now Liam won't be at my side.

Stasi and the band are it for me. Well, they *were*. Until Z.

To say all the screaming and heart-pounding adrenaline doesn't wear me out would be a lie. It is as much a mental drain as it is physical, but I won't ever air those complaints out loud. I know I'm blessed. One of the lucky ones, despite the fact that I've worked my ass off to get here, desperate to prove to my family that I'm not a complete fuck-up.

Hoping they'll admit they were wrong and welcome me back in with open arms.

And if Z decides to tour with the band when Liam's out of the picture, hell to the fucking no, I'm not calling it quits. I'll follow that man to the edge of the universe.

Backstage, I wipe the sweat from my brow on a towel thrown to me by Sondra. My thumb hovers over the send button on a group message to my parents and Max, my older brother, with the pic I took on stage.

I back out of the message and shoot the photo to Stasi instead. A few minutes later, she FaceTimes me. She's huddled up in a blanket on her apartment couch, piles of textbooks surrounding her. I can hear reality TV playing in the background.

"Hail, that is incredible," she exclaims. "Where are you tonight?"

I'm cheesing, living for the rush of her approval. Strolling into an empty dressing room, I snatch a bottle of water and a ham sandwich that was catered in hours ago. "Kansas City. We should be home next Thursday to play a show. Want to meet up for a late lunch?"

Stasi's face scrunches up. "Shoot, Hail. I have an exam and two classes that day."

My heart sinks. "No worries. Maybe a late night McDonald's drive-thru then. How about one in the morning? We can roll the windows down and blast emo music while chain-smoking. Remember how we used to do that after Mom and Dad went to bed just to feel like we had some freedom?"

This gets her to laugh. "My lungs would hate me if I smoked anything at this old age."

"Watch it, we're the same age."

She cocks a brow. "Says the twin that constantly reminds me he's two minutes older."

With a mouthful of sandwich, I reply, "Got me there."

"I'm gonna dive back into this last chapter. Miss you, bro."

"Miss you, too, Stasi. Thanks for the call."

She hangs up, and I scour the venue in search of Z, desperate to have him in sight. I shouldn't push things, but I can't help my desire to be near him. What happened in Kentucky lives rent free in my mind, replaying too often. Enough that I find myself reaching out to touch him at the most inopportune times.

Hands to yourself, Mykhail.

I find Z assisting with equipment loading. It's difficult to keep from jumping in to help, but Sondra and the crew chewed me up and down for getting in the way last time. They have their jobs, and I have mine. I'm nothing more than a hiccup in their well-oiled machine.

I perch on the edge of the stage and watch the organised madness around me while devouring my sandwich. My eyes trail Z as he works. He's coated in sweat, sickly pale and frowning. *Probably just tired.*

But then I see him sway, barely catching himself on the wall. I'm up before I can register the action. I toss my sandwich in the trash and reach out to take Z's arm in my hand.

"What's wrong?" I demand.

Images of him in his house curled over the table hit me like a sucker punch to the gut. What the fuck is happening? Is this too much for him?

I am broken. His words cycle through my head, and my protective instincts kick into overtime as I step in front of him and take his chin in my other hand.

"Nothing," Z mutters, squeezing his eyes shut to avoid my critical stare.

Cora, my guitar tech, stops next to us. Her green hair is woven into a neat braid down the center of her head, and I make a note to compliment it later. "Is he okay?" she asks, her brows furrowing. "He's been kind of out of it all night. I was worried he might be dehydrated."

Grimacing, Z pulls away from my hand and straightens up. "I'm fine."

He continues shoving the amp on wheels toward the back doors. I storm after him, blasting through the boundaries I've been striving to uphold. If this is a matter of health, though, I won't let him ignore his body's warnings.

"If you're not feeling well, you should go back to the hotel and lie down. I'll let everyone know."

He shakes his head. "Just drop it, Hail."

"Not when you look like you're about to pass out."

He sighs and faces me, desperation etched into his features. "It's nothing. Just let me do my job, okay?"

Then he rushes off, leaving me wondering what the hell I did wrong and if we'll ever get off this confusing rollercoaster of emotions.

SEVENTEEN

Z

Last night was just a fluke. A slight lapse in my brain.

I'm back on my feet after some rest. While I ended up passing out on my hotel bathroom floor last night after work, fighting through the side effects of this medication and utter denial over its failure, my brain feels stable when I wake up in the morning.

Another song flows out of me on the road to Denver. It's lighter than anything I've written, and that gives me a sliver of assurance that maybe something inside of me is finally balancing out.

I want to share my new lyrics with Hail. See how he can improve them. See what we can create together. Heart fluttering, I glance up from my notebook to find the bus already easing to a stop at the next venue.

Startled by the speed at which we arrived, I shut my notebook and tuck it away. Work comes first, above all else.

Atonement is scheduled to play a more intimate show tonight. Back when I used to perform, small places like this were my favourite. The aftermath of those shows didn't hit me so hard.

Obviously, festivals were the worst for me. Not only were the crowds massive, but the fact that some of them might not receive us well always had me throwing up before we took the stage. Not to mention the increased possibility of technical issues with such little time to prepare between performances.

My gaze snags on Hail, and I cringe at the frustration still brewing in his eyes. I'd been so lost in my little bubble of songwriting that I'd forgotten how I'd pushed him away the other night. He has every right to be upset with me.

Sneaking off the bus without exchanging words, I force my body into the routine of unloading Liam's equipment and checking all of it for damage after I haul it inside. It's become almost therapeutic to focus on cleaning, restringing, and tuning his guitars, knowing it's not me that has to go out there and bare my soul almost every night.

When it's finally time for Atonement to perform, I watch from the shadows as Hail destroys the fans with his gutturals, holding out growls so vicious, I wonder if the crumbling stone walls will come down on us. Did the engineers of the building take into account demon infestations when they designed it?

I sip at a bottle of water, eyes flitting back and forth between Liam and Hail.

What would it feel like to be on stage for a crowd like this again? My stomach lurches at the thought. Alone, I don't think I could do it, but with these guys backing me? I've never experienced support like they've shown me. Would things be different with them?

"Thank you so much, Denver!" Hail shouts into the mic. "I'd like to play you something new tonight if you're up for it. This was actually written by one of our techs. He's a very close friend of mine."

The crowd erupts and my heart sputters in my chest. He couldn't be talking about me, right? But what if he is? Dread fills my gut. *Fuck.* What is he thinking? That little comment is going to blow up online. Everyone's going to be frothing at the mouth to find out who this tech is.

Hail gives a sultry, low laugh, and electricity zings through my body like a live wire. I can't take my eyes off of him. He strides toward me to switch out his seven string guitar for an acoustic one, sneaking a kiss to my cheek.

"What are you doing?" I ask.

He just grins at me, then he grabs a stool and drags it to the centre of the stage under a single pillar of red light.

He begins to play the first song I entrusted to him. The one in the hotel room after he tended to me with such care. Confusion overtakes me. Did the other guys sign off on this? Or did they blindly trust Hail to wing it?

The melody he's written for my words is… god, it's *perfect*. He's taken something raw and polished it to a shine. When did he work on this? When I was ignoring him? Running off on my own during breaks? Late at night in hotel rooms?

Suddenly, I can't fucking breathe. My bones sit too heavy in my skin. Part of me is overwhelmed by his act of consideration. The other can't help but project Lex on that stage, strumming out my song instead of Hail, a reminder of my catastrophic failure.

No.

Whatever off-brand medication I took that morning strangles my brain and churns my stomach. Ironic that the very thing that's supposed to make me feel better—feel *normal*—is fucking throwing me for a loop right now.

Unable to hold back the chilling waves of sickness, I rush off stage and into the hall, seeking out the bathroom. Inside the paint-chipped, fluorescent room that looks like it could be a murder scene, I slam open a stall door and violently spill my guts.

"Take it easy, man!" a guy hollers from another stall.

Oh yeah, good fucking advice. I'll tell my stupid body that.

When I'm done heaving up stomach acid, I push up off my knees and wash my face with trembling hands. I peek into the dirty mirror, but I don't see myself. I see my brother. Slightly more angular features from our father's Asian-Pacific lineage. Green eyes like my mother. An actual smile.

And that's what fucking wrecks me. His *smile*.

Just when I think I've climbed out of this hole, my brain spartan kicks me back in as if to say, *remember your place.*

Flashbacks of Lex looming at the bottom of a pool crash over me. His arms weightless and hair swaying with the gentle ripples.

I burst out of the side door to the venue and call a cab, not trusting my body to hold me all the way back to the hotel we booked for the evening, and not sure what I plan to do about the fucking ghost in my head.

I only know that I need to forget him. To forget it's entirely my fault that he's dead.

Eighteen

Hail

Hope withers in my chest as I pace by Z's hotel door, frantically checking my phone to make sure he hasn't texted me or called me back after several attempts to reach him.

What the hell happened? I thought the song would be a good surprise. Thought he'd be moved by it. I worked hard on the melody, certain I'd gotten it right.

Did someone upset him during the show? If Z needs me to go after somebody, I'll fucking do it. I'm not an angry person, but when it comes to him, I don't know that there's anything I wouldn't do to keep his shattered pieces somewhat intact.

Liam catches me on my thirtieth lap up and down the halls. Calming my racing heart, I shoot for a laid back expression as I give him a little nod. "Sup."

"You trying to wear a path in the carpet?" he asks, eyes drifting to the number on the wall beside Z's door.

"Just...couldn't sleep. Too amped up after tonight's performance."

"Have you talked to him?" Liam asks, crossing his arms and leaning against his door.

My shoulders droop on a heavy sigh. "No, not yet. You're not going to fire him, are you?"

"With him ditching out on a show like that? Normally, I would. I've dropped techs for less."

My forehead bangs against Z's door. "I know. *Fuck.*"

This is my fault for pressuring Z into this situation. It has to be my fault. He wouldn't even be here if not for me. I hope he didn't assume I was upset with him last night. I was just worried about him, that's all.

"Cora tracked me down and told me Z hasn't been feeling well. She had to carry extra weight to cover for him, but she wouldn't have done that if she didn't care about him. He's earned respect among the crew. So no, I'm not going to fire him tonight."

All I can do is nod and sniffle. When my gaze cuts back to Liam, he rubs at his jaw. "Look, Hail—"

Here it comes. Typical Liam lecture full of logic and wisdom, and I don't fucking want it. I don't.

"I'm not going to tell you how to live your life. You're a grown ass man. But that guy? He's haunted. I would hate to see you get dragged down into a bad place because of him."

I open my mouth, ready to go to bat for Z, but Liam cuts in. "Not that he would intentionally hurt you. I just... want you to think carefully about what you're doing. For your sake and his."

Terror grips me. Part of me wants to lash out that he doesn't know a thing, but Liam lost his father to alcoholism after surviving a childhood of abuse. It's why he still can't seem to settle into a healthy relationship, only chasing sex from strangers.

If anyone has an eye for monsters invisible to the rest of us, it's Liam.

"Just be careful with your heart, okay? You've got a good one," he says, vanishing into his room. The click of the door kick starts my worried heart into overdrive again.

Still at war with myself about what to do to help, I stride up to Z's door and bang on it. A few unsteady breaths later, no answer.

The worst case scenarios play out in my head, ushering me down the stairwell at lightning speed because the elevator was too fucking slow.

I reach the front desk and demand a replacement key. Both rooms are booked under my name, so guest services hands one over, and then I'm bounding back up the stairs.

Swiping the key over the lock, I barge into Z's room. Darkness greets me. Not even a glow from a TV. I hear the shower running, but no light shines out from under the door. Dread convinces me that I'll find him in a state like I did in his house in London.

"Z?" I call out, my pulse thundering as I knock on the bathroom door.

No response. Holding my breath, I slowly turn the handle and flick on the hallway switch. Light bleeds into the bathroom, illuminating Z curled up on the damp tiles, drenched and trembling.

What. The. Fuck.

I rush over to him, my knees smacking down on the tiles. My heart slams against my ribs, convinced I'm about to lose him for good. Which isn't fucking fair because I just found him.

Brushing curls out of his eyes, I confirm that he's awake and aware of his surroundings. Silent tears leak down his face.

"Z." My voice tremors. "What is going on with you?" I cradle him against me, striving to bleed life and warmth back into his cold, wet body. "You've gotta talk to me, okay? Just... just tell me what's wrong."

His fingers grip my shirt over my sternum, clutching at me like he's about to slip off a ledge or sink into the depths of the ocean. He lets out a sob so gutting, I feel pieces of myself cracking with him.

Dropping down onto my butt, I pull him half onto my lap and hold him for god knows how long until he stops shaking and wailing and clawing at his temples like there's something burned into his brain he can't get out.

All I can do is clutch him tight and rest my chin on his head. "Please talk to me. Tell me how to help."

He doesn't say anything, and my eyes flick up to the counter where I see another bottle of medication. The label is some off-brand antidepressant. Panic tears through me like a wildfire after a drought as I recall how much shit Liam suffered through. How close I was to losing him before he found the proper therapist to guide him through hell. Hot tears well in my eyes, and I have a moment of doubt. Maybe I should listen to Liam and guard my heart.

I fucking wash that horrible thought right down the drain. Z has no one to care. No one to fight for him besides me. Who gives a fuck about a little shrapnel in my heart? I'm not going to kick him aside when he's already wounded.

My hand rests against his damp cheek, and he lets me guide his head up until our eyes meet.

"How do I help?" I plead. "Give me the name of your demons, and I will slaughter them all."

As if it were that easy. I know for a fact it's not. As much as I want to *will* hope back into his body, it's ultimately up to him to find it again. But saying those words gives me the illusion of power.

He tugs at my shirt, bringing me close enough to breathe onto his lips. "Help me forget."

And then he kisses me. It takes me a moment to lose myself in the feel of his lips against mine. I debate pulling away, knowing he's not in a good place right now, uncertain if this is a side effect of antidepressants or something stronger.

But if this is what he needs, if this is what he's asking for...

I break away, though I keep my mouth hovering over his. "Z—"

"You want to stay or not? I know what I'm asking for. I'm sober, just messed the fuck up from that medication. All I need is a distraction. Please distract me."

My heart speeds up, and it doesn't take much more persuasion from his mouth before I'm parting his lips with my tongue and running it against his own. If he wants me to bring him back to life, so be it. I'll get his blood flowing. I'll make him forget whatever horrors plague him.

Dick straining in my pants, I carefully switch our positions until I'm sitting atop his hips and his back is plastered to the wet floor. I don't bother shutting off the stream of water. It'll help cover up the moans of pleasure I'm about to wring from his body.

We get to work ripping clothes off each other, and I take time to marvel at his smooth skin. He's all lean muscle. It's such a stark contrast to the size of his dick when I finally tug it out of his boxers.

"Christ, Z. I love your body."

Gripping his cock, I give it a few long, slow strokes. He's fighting to get my shirt off, exposing muscle and ink. He seems to enjoy tracing both with his calloused fingers and warm tongue.

My free hand clutches him by the hair. As I lean back up, I draw him with me, keeping his mouth fixed to my pierced nipple. I growl, shocked by the need throbbing in my rock-hard dick.

With surprising strength, he holds my weight as he crawls us back against the wall, leaning me against it. His hands work to pop open my jeans and strip them off.

Soon, we're both naked and panting and damp from the water pooled on the tile floor. I've never destroyed a hotel room before, but I'm prepared to do it tonight and foot the bill.

I stare into his eyes with reverence and a little uncertainty. "I've never done this..."

With a guy.

I don't get to finish. He lowers his mouth to my dick, and I'm fucking molten beneath him, wriggling as his tongue strokes over me and his hands spread my thighs.

"Ah, fuck." I grab his damp locks as he slides up and down my length, hitting too many nerves all at once. He takes me deep, and I groan. "That's so good. So *fucking* good, Z."

Not wanting this to be over too quickly, I hook an arm around his waist and shift us until it's his back against the wall and me encroaching on his space, nipping and sucking at his perfect lips, salty from my precum. "I'm going to blow if you keep doing that."

He gives a sly little grin that has my heart lurching in my chest. I'm so screwed. I want to brand my name into his skin. Claim him as mine. Keep him locked up forever.

I run my tongue over the crown of his dick, not surprised at all that I enjoy the taste of him. The feel of him. The jerk of his cock against my mouth as I suck him off. He's so turned on, and that makes me ache harder for release.

Popping off, I ask, "What do you need, Z?"

"Lube," he demands, panting. "Front pocket of my backpack."

Well, hot damn. I probably would have had a nosebleed if I had spotted that in his backpack, knowing how I felt about him the moment I first laid eyes on him. Knowing I had to be inside of him the moment his words infected me in that underground London bar.

Rushing for his bag outside the bathroom, I rifle through each compartment, not wanting to lose the moment. Or him. *Jesus, don't think about this being a one-time thing.*

Finding the lube, I scurry back into the bathroom and nearly wipe out on the slick tile. I drop to my knees between his spread legs, groaning as I get a full view of him, legs spread, lean stomach muscles flexed, dark hair hanging down over his stunning eyes, and heavy dick clutched in his hand. His other hand dips to tug on his balls.

Anticipation has my pulse running faster than a live show. I squirt lube into my palm and suck in a deep breath, absorbing the vision of him, disheveled and needy for me.

No, he just wants an escape. Not me.

"Are you... seeing anyone else?" I ask hesitantly, wondering if I took action too soon, hand covered in lube.

He shakes his head. "No. It's been years."

"Okay." I nod. "For me too."

It dawns on me that I haven't actually slept with anyone since my ex, which was what, three years ago? Fuck, I'm horrible at this metal god thing.

My brows furrow. "Should I still get a condom?"

He shakes his head, tongue darting out to wet his lips. "I want you bare."

His eyes watch my hand as I lower it between his legs and circle a hesitant finger around his hole. He tips his head back in pleasure, and I gain confidence, sometimes letting my hand drift up to stroke his cock before I slide it back down to rub at him.

I want eternity to learn what he likes. How to set him the fuck off.

Sinking a finger inside of him, my own orgasm threatens to unleash at this delicious act alone.

"God damn, you're tight. Are you sure about this?"

He blinks those long, dark lashes at me, his ice-blue eyes bewitching me. "I can take you, Koval."

Another finger slides in, pushing and stretching and ruining me for everything else. Everyone else.

Wasting no time, I scoot closer to move the head of my dick along his crease, watching in rapture of this lude act. So painfully slow, I begin to push inside of him, groaning at the hot grip of his body. I clutch the towel rack above our heads, my other hand holding his hip, fingers pressing into the soft flesh of his round ass.

"Fuck, I might be an ass man." *Quite literally.* I'm buried halfway inside of Z. He fights back a wince, and I pause. "Z."

His hands grab my ass and haul me all the way inside of him. And, oh god, my eyes shudder as we both release moans. I lean over him, pressing kisses and whispered curses against his collarbone and neck and perfect lips.

As I start moving my hips, I swallow up the little noises he makes and feed him my own primal growls. He tilts my hips to help me pinpoint his prostate.

"God, right there. Yes."

"I'm too close already," I murmur, worried he'll be disappointed in my endurance.

He raises up to bring his mouth to my ear, setting off flutters in my stomach. "Finish inside of me."

"*Fuck.*" I shiver and unload on another hard pump, grateful the shower is running to muffle our noises. Though, I'm sure they can still be heard from outside the room.

His cock twitches against me, and I glance down to see that his stomach's already coated in his own release. I give him a gentle kiss because I feel like that's the respectful thing to do after I just wrecked him.

And I don't ever want to stop kissing him.

Stretching a hand under the stream of water in the shower, I grimace at the lukewarm temperature. "Do hotels run out of hot water?"

"I suppose I've been running it for a while," he replies, brushing locks of hair from his face.

I hoist him onto his feet, eyes roving over him in appreciation. "That's okay. You're enough heat for me."

His laugh is soft like him, and I'm fucking smitten when he presses a kiss to the corner of my jaw. "Thank you."

I swallow, my chest rising and falling too fast. "Sure thing, Z."

"You don't have to stay. I'm okay now."

Anger rises up within me. He can't even support his body fully. Ignoring his words, I grip him by the waist and ease us both into the shower. When I glance back up at his face, I see tears spilling down his cheeks. My face scrunches up in worry, but he just shakes his head. I don't know when his tears will stop, but I'm not leaving until they do.

"Was this because I played your song on stage?" I ask.

He shakes his head, wet locks swaying. "I think it was a culmination of things. This has been the most I've been off my... routine. Traveling overseas. Spending time with all of you. And then witnessing how you turned my words into something incredible on stage. It made me feel... guilty."

"Guilty over what, Z?" I turn him around and pull his back against my chest under the spray of water. My arms lock tightly around him, supporting some of his weight.

"I can't..." He shakes his head furiously, and I nuzzle my head into his neck, pressing lingering kisses there.

"Okay," I whisper, grateful for even the little sliver of him he's offered me. "I can respect that."

Once we're scrubbed clean and dressed in fresh boxers, we move to his bed. I don't even ask, just climb under the blankets. He sprawls his long body over my waist, and I can't help but give his full ass a satisfying squeeze.

"This view is not helping me relax," I admit.

His head tilts around until he's looking back at me with those fucking inno-cent eyes. We stay like that for a while, memorizing each other. Occasionally, I brush light fingers through his hair or over his cheekbone.

"Why dragons?" he asks softly, fingers trailing the lines of ink up my ribs.

I'm happy to give up details of my life if it's a distraction from whatever haunts him. "I don't know. I guess I thought they'd bring me good luck. Some-thing about the two different dragons, one black and one white, settled with me when I spotted them. Like it's me fighting against the doubtful, critical part of my brain. And they look badass."

He rolls his eyes on a soft laugh.

Eventually, we switch on the TV, drawn into watching *John Wick 4*.

"There is no way he could live after falling down that many stairs," I mutter, my fingers toying with locks of his hair.

Z chuckles. "If that's the only unrealistic thing you're going to call out in this movie, then there's something wrong with you."

I ruffle his hair, and he nips at my stomach.

"You mesmerize me," he says, kissing where he bit me.

I suck in a breath, feeling my dick thickening for another round. All he has to do is blow air in my general direction and I'm turned on. "Is that why you keep hanging around?"

Z crawls up my body, looming over me. My throat constricts as my heart thumps heavily. "That, and my job." His nose scrunches. "If I even have a job anymore."

My expression contorts in union with the sharp cut of pain in my chest. "I talked to Liam. He understands."

Z frowns. "He shouldn't. He needs someone reliable."

Then his mouth is on mine. We take our time, swapping slow, tender kisses, wholly in the moment while John Wick pops off a few hundred people behind us.

I run my hands up his perfect body, needing more of his silky skin. More of him. More of his heart. Whatever he can give me. I hook fingers into the waistband of his underwear and drag them down. Quickly kicking off the blankets and my own boxers, I pull him closer until our dicks rest against each other, giving me delicious pressure and an image I'll be jacking off to for the rest of my life.

"God, this is insane. I don't think I can get enough of you, Z," I say, heart beating rapidly against my ribcage.

His smile is genuine, and I can't help but flip him over, straddling his hips. His gaze on me is heated, his body wriggling beneath me.

"So eager. Do you like when I take charge?" I ask, my voice low and deep with lust.

"Yes," he whispers, his eyelids fluttering.

"Good. And you like it when I take you into my mouth?" I lower between his knees and bob most of the way down his dick.

He moans in approval. "Yes."

I suction as hard as I can when I rise back up, swirling my tongue over his tip. I don't have a lot of experience with this, but I'll make up for it with effort.

"Ughhh." He trembles beneath me. I have never felt more powerful than in this moment. Screw manipulating the emotions of hundreds of thousands of fans. Here is where I reign supreme, with Z underneath me, driven to the edge as I pleasure him.

I fumble for the lube I set on the nightstand, slicking both of our dicks in my hand. It doesn't take long before we're both crushing our bodies together, chasing something neither of us is going to get. I want his whole heart and he just wants to be whole.

My forehead rests on his as I reach my limit, slowing the roll of my hips as pressure builds and builds at the base of my spine. Muscles spasm, and then I'm unloading warm strands of cum onto his stomach.

I take his dick in both hands and work him in tandem until his release shoots up onto his chest. *Jesus, that's hot.*

"Hail," he murmurs, tipping his head back as he rides out his orgasm.

He. Is. Destroying. Me.

I plop my body down on his, bracing some of my weight on my forearms and knees, unconcerned about the cum sticking us together.

We lay there until the credits for the movie roll. Proceeding to shower all over again, this time in steaming water, we make out some more, though neither of us has the energy to take things further.

Then I tuck him into bed beside me and watch him fall asleep on my bicep.

I can't let him go, even after our tour is over. But how do I get him to stay with me when it feels like he's got one foot in the grave?

I dream of the ocean.

Cold. Expansive. Deadly. Floating in its turbulent, unforgiving body, I swim for land. I swim and swim and swim, but I never get closer. Never escape the waves that crash over me.

If there is a god, he gets off on torture.

Hail crawls out of bed too fucking early, planting a quick kiss on the corner of my mouth. We don't talk about what happened the night before, and I have no interest in being alive at this unholy hour on one of our rare days that set up doesn't start until late morning. So I roll back over and try to fall into a nightmare-less sleep.

When I finally make up my mind to stop being lazy and work on songs instead, I peel my sore body out of bed. Thank god my head no longer feels bogged down.

Dressed in black joggers and a clean white t-shirt, I float down to breakfast to find Atonement and their crew destroying the buffet line. Hotel staff can't keep enough food out to satisfy their hunger, and I notice Liam slipping them tips for the hassle.

"Okay, but if a bear charged in here right now, right this fucking minute, you're telling me you think you could escape uninjured?" Malek's huddled over his stack of pancakes, his attention focused on Griff.

Griff rubs both hands over his stubbled head. "Absolutely, dude. I'd jump up on that counter and shimmy into the air return, then caterpillar my way the fuck right out of here. No problem."

Liam snorts. "Okay, Mission Impossible."

"I don't need your sass, Liam. I was up most of the night listening to you pound into that fangirl through the thin wall." Griff stuffs his mouth with eggs.

Liam stretches back in his chair. "Much more enjoyable than plotting bear escapes, in my opinion."

Griff snaps his head back to Malek. "Anywho. Your plan for surviving inevitable bear attacks should one break through that window?"

Malek scoffs, waving his fork around with a chunk of pancake on it. "Easy. I'd ninja star those ceramic plates at its face. Then I'd pull out one of those buffet pans and start banging on it. Bears hate loud noises."

"Wouldn't that just piss it off?" Hail chimes in, running a hand down his content stomach. I'm too stunned by this rapid, high-energy exchange to do anything more than sip at a cup of tea and pick at some toast and glance over at Liam to gauge how pissed he is at me for my inexcusable absence at the venue last night.

"Y'all's conversations baffle me. Is this the shit that circulates the male brain all day?" Sondra butts in, spearing a piece of fruit.

"Ninety-five percent of the male brain is dedicated to planning for worst case scenarios, Sondra. You'll thank us one day when we save your life," Griff answers.

"Yeah, Sondra," Malek adds with a dramatic eye roll, though his focus hasn't left Griff. I wonder at the undercurrent of chemistry I detect there. Just a strong friendship or something more?

"Sondra, we love you." Hail makes a heart with his hands in her direction and she flips everyone off.

"Z, what did you do to piss her off this morning?" Malek taunts, sucking down half a glass of orange juice.

I burn red hot with shame, wondering just how far word spread about me bailing on work. How quickly I'll be out of a job. How will I get back to London? I doubt Sondra will book a flight for me this time.

Liam stands and walks behind me, his hand ruffling my hair. "Don't sweat it, kid. Glad to see you're feeling better."

And that's it. Everything I've been stressed about melts away. No scathing looks. No screaming. No threatening.

Feeling confused but also somewhat empty, I slip away from the breakfast madness to explore a nearby park, notepad and guitar in hand. It's mostly barren, probably due to the heat advisory, but I don't mind the delicious burn on my skin. It's nice to experience weather that isn't so miserable all the time, a staple in England.

Instead of being productive, I end up laid out in a grassy field watching masses of thick clouds drift overhead while music plays in my headphones.

I try to sort out how I feel about last night. Not only did I scare the shit out of Hail with all my baggage, but I took something I never should have taken from him. I allowed a connection to solidify between us when I knew this could never just be sex with him.

Nothing can ever be simple for my brain, but I need him to understand that this cannot be permanent.

My phone buzzes in my pocket, interrupting the song playing. I lift it to see another message from my mum pop up.

Why haven't you sent money? J. Flowers keeps calling me about a past due balance.

There's missed calls from the artists I signed contracts with, too. Sighing, I slide my phone back into my pocket and squeeze my eyes closed. *I haven't sent you money because I have no more money to send. Not until I get another paycheck. I'm hanging on by a fucking thread and you keep tugging, and one day soon we're both going to fucking unravel like we were always destined to do.*

When my mum started me in music lessons, the agreement was I would pay her back. I know I've well exceeded that debt, but she keeps asking, and I keep giving. Guilt is a strong motivator.

The last time she actually had a long conversation with me was when Visage's first song went big. She called me to remind me how costly it was to raise me and my brother, Lex. How she was barely surviving on a single income. How my father left us because of my selfish decisions.

Songwriting became more about survival than freedom and self-expression. The pressure led me to my first encounter with drugs. Just to take the edge off. Soon that edge turned into a cliff I needed to overcome just to function.

I'm all mum has now. I'm the reason she's so unwell. And while she doesn't care to ever see me again, she will at least accept my money. That has to be enough.

I switch to my classical playlist, the one that helps me navigate the mottled net of emotions in my chest. Lyrics begin to float through my mind, and I do my best to capture them in my notebook.

I am shattered cathedral glass

Do you remember how you used to worship?

Before your hands became so ruthless

Rearranging me into crystal pieces

You won't stop until I turn to dust

My phone buzzes again, only this time it's Hail.

Where you at?

I type a message and erase it a half dozen times. I shouldn't allow the distraction. Shouldn't give him any faith that we could ever have something more than a professional relationship.

Stupidly, I respond with my location. He's probably just checking on me. Making sure I haven't bailed again like I always do. No need to send him into a panic when we both need to maintain a level head.

Sometime into my playlist, a shadow darkens the red glow of sunlight behind my closed eyelids.

"You often fall asleep in parks?" Hail asks, and it takes me a few blinks up at him to realise he's real. This is not a conjuring in my head. He really is my worst nightmare and my most delightful dream, all wrapped up in one handsome body. Everything he is, my internal animal agrees with.

Hitting pause on my playlist, I ask, "Is it time to set up already?"

He frowns and checks his phone. "Considering it's only ten, I hope not."

Already ten? Did I disassociate so hard that I fucking travelled through time? How have I only accomplished writing a few lines when I owe so many artists a chunk of my no-good, tattered soul?

Hail plops down beside me and steals a wireless headphone. He reaches an arm over my body to hit play on my phone, then snuggles up next to me in the soft grass.

I can't keep my eyes off him. I watch every little shift in his features, in awe of this perfect human. His is something good. Pure. Unearthly.

I will surely break him.

"Classical," he murmurs, closing his eyes. "Knew it. Did you take lessons?"

"It became the only thing for me."

"Same. Probably why I failed out of classes senior year. I didn't actually graduate," Hail admits. His head rolls to the side to meet my watchful eyes for judgment. "It tore my family up pretty good. Or I should say, it damaged their reputation."

My brows furrow, a dull pain spreading through my chest. "Do you miss them?"

"Sometimes. Sometimes I wonder if I just miss the idea of family. I send my mom messages occasionally, but they go unanswered. Stasi and I talk sporadically. I think it's Max I really miss. He's my oldest sibling. I tagged along with him constantly when we were kids."

His growing frown gives tell to how that relationship progressed. "What happened?"

Hail sighs and gazes up at the drifting, fluffy clouds. "Nothing happened. I became an embarrassment. Didn't like me hanging around his elitist friends.

Even when I proved myself with music, it didn't change anything because I wasn't playing the *right* type of music. And now look at me."

He motions lazily over his body. My gaze trails down and then back up to meet his eyes once more. I let every bit of admiration bleed out into my next words. "I'm looking, Hail."

His Adam's apple bobs when he turns his head to face me. His teeth sink into his bottom lip as he scoots close enough that our arms press together. He tips his chin enough that his lips are a breath away.

Logic tells me to stay away. To protect him.

But sensing his need for intimacy, I close the small distance between us and press my mouth softly to his. We kiss through the remainder of my playlist, never taking things beyond the careful movement of our lips and tongues mapping each other, slow and warm and mind-numbing.

His pinkie finger curls around mine, and I'm hooked on this expanding, heated, fluttery feeling all over my body. Better than any drug I've taken.

When the music switches to something jarringly pop, I break away. Hail's smile is sweet, his eyes warm pools of honey. I'm glad we're in a public place, or I'd be tempted to climb on top of him and ride him right here.

I hand him my phone with the Spotify app open. "Pick something you like."

Rapid fingers type, and I snuggle my head into the crook of his neck to glimpse him spelling out Jinjer, a band I've never heard before. Instantly, I'm enchanted by a stylistic, feminine voice. When she starts into soul-shattering screams, I can't help but chuckle. "What *is* this?"

"Talent," Hail replies with a smirk. "She's one of my favourites."

We fall into an effortless rhythm, taking turns passing my phone back and forth. He introduces me to a French band called Gojira. I'm perplexed by the skill of their drummer and the melodic tone of the vocalist as he screams. Then I share an FKJ song with him, enjoying the tapping of his fingers on the back of my hand and the little bobs of his head to the jazzy, rhythmic beat.

"It's good." He smiles. "We should swap music more often."

My heart sinks a bit at the comment. There will come a day when we don't share anything. No lyrics. No music. No heated glances. No kisses.

While last night was the most intimate I've been with anyone in a long time, this right here, this brief moment in time, will live on forever in my heart.

Hail's phone rings, startling him out of our little peaceful bubble in the centre of the park.

"Yeah, we're headed back."

I can hear Sondra chewing him out on the other end, but can't make out her words. Sighing, I watch him roll up onto his feet and ruffle his hair awkwardly. I don't make a move from my spot, though I can sense he wants something from me. I don't have the courage to ask what though.

"Come on, sunshine. Back to the grind for us." His eyes shimmer with hope.

I exist only to crush it.

I make a habit of sending Z texts because I'm a child that can't be left alone.

I barrage his phone with messages about how we all appreciate him. How cute he looks when he's running around backstage like a madman. How much I think about kissing him all hours of the day.

Sometimes I send him spicy things to see if he'll read them while on set. I enjoy imagining what his expressions are, too. The mystery excites me more than a fresh brewed cup of coffee hitting my senses in the wee hours of the morning.

He never reads them at work anymore, caught on to my mischief, and I always pout about it. But while he's never one to talk much in person, I think he enjoys communicating through written word because he always takes the time to respond to each one of my texts in our downtime, even if we're together.

Arriving back at the venue after lunch with the boys—Malek and Griff have been more clingy than usual—I shoot off a message to Z.

Good morning, sunshine.

His response comes surprisingly quick. Maybe he didn't go back to the hotel to nap on his break, sneaking off for some peace and quiet instead. I tend to be overbearing, but I've been trying to give him *some* space. Minimal, more like.

Is that my nickname now?

I think it might be.

It doesn't suit me.

I can't help a sly grin as my focus goes to my phone, drawn away from the commotion around me. I bump into equipment and somebody's shoulder. I think it might have been Malek, but who really cares?

That's one guy's opinion, I fire back. *I think it's a perfect fit.*

If I have to have a nickname, so do you.

I'm all ears. Or eyes in this case, because you know... texting. Unless you want to wait to tell me in person. Just be prepared for the consequences.

Three little dots appear, and my heart skips a beat. *Consequences?*

I'm grinning like a lovesick fool. *Probably something sexual.*

There's a long pause before his response comes through. *I'll wait, then.*

Fighting to keep my groan trapped behind my teeth, my finger hovers over the FaceTime button. Fuck, I really shouldn't. I need to tamp down on this desire for him when I should be thinking about performing.

Except, this might be the first time I don't actually want to play a show. Regardless of how drained I've become of screaming into people's ears for a solid two hours, music is the one thing I have in life. My one hobby. My one investment I've sunk all of my time and effort into.

I can't just want to give that up, can I?

No, I don't think I do. I just want... I want him, too.

Slipping down a hallway, I find an empty dressing room. I shut the door behind me and keep the light off as I hit the button to call Z. My heart beats rapidly at the anticipation of seeing him and hearing his deep, low voice, so at odds with his lean build.

He answers on the third ring, still face down on his hotel bed, shirtless and disheveled. God, I want to run my hands all over his glorious, pale, smooth skin.

"Hey, sunshine," I whisper around a grin. I get a grunted response, which makes me chuckle. "Rough morning?"

"Dropped an amp on my toe and suffered from a bit of writer's block," he admits, turning his head to the camera. He cracks an eye, and I'm speechless for a moment as I take him in. A curious blue iris like the clearest pool of water. Dark lashes and straight, full brows. Tendrils of dark hair curled over his forehead and down his temples.

"Did you call just to stare at me?" he asks. The little upward curl of his perfect mouth has my dick hardening in my tight jeans. Not the ideal situation in a venue about to be full of crew members again.

"I didn't, but tell me you don't love it."

Z's smile is timid as he closes his eyes. When he rolls onto his back, he flips the camera to give me a full view of his toned stomach and the noticeable stiffness in his low-riding sweatpants.

I growl. "Fuck. Why am I not there to take care of that?"

"Because you're off being social and loved by your bandmates."

I grind my teeth together and palm my stiffening cock. "Take it out. Show me."

"You sure about that?" His voice is sultry and low, still full of sleep. Oh, I like post-nap Z far too much. He's in for a hell of a lot more wake-up calls, next time in person. I'll kick his door down and drop a check for the damages on the manager's desk.

Running a hand through my hair and tugging at the ends, I reply, "So fucking sure, sunshine. Take your cock out and stroke it for me right now."

Z hooks a thumb in his waistband. "You ever been edged before, Hails?"

My brows furrow. "What?"

Z flips the camera to his grinning face. "Enjoy your show."

And then he hangs up on me.

I can't help but let out a sharp laugh that echoes in the space. My dick is still hard, straining against the tight fabric of my black pants. I pace until I get myself calmed back down enough to exit the dressing room, knowing I'll be all worked up again come time for soundcheck.

Punishment is coming, Z, I text back.

Z and I write a few solid songs together during the late evenings and early mornings we're on the road. When Malek and Griff start whining about being lonely, we all play collectively. I know Z enjoys it, regardless of how quickly he vanishes into his shell when we're done. Like, slowly, we're all providing the mortar to his cracked foundation.

Hope continues to blossom in my chest that he might actually consider taking Liam's spot at the end of the tour. I know Malek and Griff want that, too, from their little glances back and forth when they hear him tear through riffs.

And the nights we stay in a hotel? Z and I secretly end up in the same room, though we haven't engaged in any illicit behavior since the bathroom floor incident. He's doubled down on his iron walls, but I'm patient. I'll win him over with overpriced DoorDash, shitty movies, and flirty texts.

This little sliver of normalcy has become something I live for when work requires us to go all the time. I honestly don't know how Liam has the energy to work out. We do enough cardio on stage.

Z and I are watching some low-budget horror movie called *Swamp Ape* as the bus rolls into Dallas, too exhausted from playing back-to-back shows to engage in any activity that involves excessive movement or brain activity.

Liam took a phone call and bailed out in his Pantera at the last gas station. I shouldn't be surprised. We're finally in our hometown. He's probably got another hook-up or two waiting for him. That's how Liam's been since middle school. He was three years older than everyone else, having been held back a couple of times in elementary school due to some trouble with reading. Though I know the real reason was because of his home life interfering with his focus.

The first time I asked him if he'd ever consider giving a long-term relationship a try, he told me he's never witnessed what a healthy relationship looks like.

While Liam fills the hole inside of him with meaningless sex, I've avoided it entirely. But I can't lie and say I'm not a bit jealous that Liam has some connections here. Other than the occasional conversation with Stasi, I don't really communicate with anyone outside the band.

I messaged Stasi about meeting up for dinner or lunch or whatever she has time for while we're in town, but she left me on read, which makes me wonder if she's ignoring me because of our parents or because she actually doesn't want to see me. Or maybe I'm just being annoying and she's busy with college, like she told me.

Peeking over at Z on the couch, I can't help but want to corrupt him. I've never seen a rockstar or metalhead without a piercing or tattoo. Z has none that I've seen, and I've searched over every inch of his skin.

My gaze lingers on the delicate shape of his ear beneath inky curls of hair. I drink in his flawless moonlit skin, his perfect fucking profile, and the smooth column of his neck.

He's ethereal. He reminds me of Kaname Kuran from Vampire Knight, a manga my sister used to read. Hell, I even got sucked in, trying to mold my image after the characters when I believed that's what girls liked.

Who knew I'd be more interested in what guys liked? Or is it just Z that does it for me? It doesn't really matter because he's the only one that matters.

Shit, am I smitten already? Liam always teased me for falling hard and fast. Nothing I can do to stop it at this point, except figure out how to keep Z in my life for good.

Spurred on by a wild thought, I Google the nearest piercing parlor when we pull into the back of the hotel parking lot. Malek leans over my shoulder on his way to grab another beer. I shove at his head, but he comes right back like a rubber band.

"Creeper," I accuse him.

"Are we getting a tattoo?" he asks excitedly.

Griff perks up from his sketchpad at the small table. "Fuck yeah!"

"Liam's going to be pissed we left him out," Malek says.

"Liam ditched us for pussy. Screw him," Griff replies.

"For real, though, we hittin' that place up?" Malek continues, rolling up his sleeve to show off his pale bicep. "I have an idea of what I need to fill this space."

Z's been tuned out this entire conversation. I nudge him with my shoe, and he lifts his head to me, brows furrowed.

I flash him a devilish grin. "Let's go put a hole in that ear."

"Mine?" His voice comes out high-pitched.

"And mine." I rise up from the couch and clasp a hand around his forearm. Drawing him up, probably too close, I lean in next to his ear. "We can get matching ones."

When I step back, his throat bobs. Though he doesn't refuse, which is enough permission for me to orchestrate this little pit stop. We load in the black rental SUV after I snatch the keys from Sondra, smirking at her warning to behave.

Soon, we're standing in the fluorescent-lit lobby of the shop, Z at my side, looking drained of blood.

I brush my fingers over the back of his hand. "Hey, if you don't want to…"

He shakes his head, eyeing the jewelry in the glass case. "S'fine."

"No pressure or anything."

"I want one." He looks up at me with flushed cheeks. "If you're getting one, too."

Fuck. My chest swells, and my stupid heart thumps happily at the idea of something shared between us. Something permanent.

We agree on a silver hoop with a delicate chain that ends in a cross. I'm already sporting a half chub imagining what he'll look like with the gothic piece in place.

Z sits down in the red vinyl chair first, and I give his hand a squeeze. He tenses up as the needle spears his cartilage. Then he looks up at me with those wide, glacial eyes, seeking approval.

"Shit. I think I found a new religion," I whisper, gaze moving from the cross piercing that gives him an edge down to his tempting, parted lips.

"No making out in public!" Malek shouts.

Z's cheeks flush rosy pink, and I take a moment to decipher how I feel about the others discovering just how close we really are. When I settle on *don't care*, I take Z's jaw in one hand and press my mouth against his, instantly awakening hot need in my core.

Griff whistles and Malek starts in on PDA, which is ironic because he's the most guilty of us all. He's been photographed in way too many compromising positions in public settings.

I don't know what I expected, but I'm pleasantly surprised when no one seems a bit phased by our demonstration.

"You all know I was bi or something?" I ask, unable to hide my smirk as I keep my eyes on Z's pretty mouth.

"Nah, but it's all good, man," Malek replies. "Even I can admit that Z's fucking hot."

Z flushes bright red all over again, then I drop into the seat, prepared to tie myself to him in any way possible.

"We're short an opener," Sondra informs us backstage. She paces in front of where the band has perched on mismatched chairs and equipment, her heels clacking with purpose as her fingers dance across her cellphone. "Of all places, it had to happen in Dallas. Our hometown, for fuck's sake!"

"It's all good," Hail says calmly. "We can just go out early and play a longer show. We can spin this to keep the fans happy."

From the lack of enthusiasm in his tone, I can tell he doesn't want to play an extended set. All the members of Atonement are growing weary, just over midway through their US tour after spending months in Europe.

"Absolutely not. You haven't finished warming up." Sondra shakes her sleek ponytail back and forth. "We can't risk you damaging your vocal cords. We're booked up for another two months."

Hail sighs, fingers drumming on the wobbly stool he's acquired. "Shouldn't the talent manager or venue manager make an announcement?"

My eyes sweep out to the noisy crowd, probably several drinks into their night. They're crammed in against the metal barriers so tight, I can already sense trouble brewing. Security is on high alert.

"They're scrambling through decisions. The crowd is getting restless," Sondra complains.

Not hard to figure out why. We rolled up to the venue early in the morning and hardcore fans were already camped out, snaking around the brick exterior of the venue half a mile down the street. Security had to help escort us all in and out of the back doors as fans screeched to get the band's attention.

Stomach churning, I step out of the shadows. The words are out of my mouth before I register what I'm doing. "How long?"

Five sets of wide eyes fall on me. I shift my weight between my hips as my pulse quickens. I keep my focus on Sondra, even though Hail's the one that responds first. "Thirty minutes tops."

"Okay." I nod. "I'll do it. I'll open for you."

It's the first time I've seen Sondra at a loss for words. If I hadn't partaken in jam sessions, she probably would have shut down my offer immediately. Instead, Sondra lifts her phone to her ear.

"Yeah, Jimmy? I have a solid replacement. Thirty-minute set. We can still offer refunds if fans want them, but if I'm not being too bold here, I think everyone came to see Atonement, not the opening act."

We wait in tense silence while Jimmy mumbles something on the other end. Then Sondra's jabbing a finger at my chest. "You're on, Z. Knock 'em dead."

Malek cracks a smile. "Get ready, boys! This one's going down in history."

Liam grabs one of his guitars and goes to work, slinging the strap over my shoulder and hooking me up. Then he pats my cheek. "You've got this. Proud of you."

My chest heaves at those three fucking words. They wield such power over me, I'm almost nailed to the spot, waiting for him to feed me more encouragement.

Hail's hands grip my biceps. He gives me a quick kiss right there in front of everyone backstage. No one bats an eye. "You're amazing. You're going to blow their minds. Just do what you did in Selma's bar and at soundchecks, and you'll have them all eating out of the palm of your hand, I just know it. Do you want me in the front row?"

"That would defeat the whole purpose of me going out there, Hails," I say, unable to hold back a nervous chuckle.

Heart pounding like it's going to explode, I step out under the warm spotlights and face the crowd. Memories slam into me. Suddenly, I panic that I might choke on them. My stomach churns. My eyes close against the harsh lights and the sea of boisterous people, crammed in like sardines in a can.

Don't think about sardines right now. You cannot puke on Hail's fans.

I'd always been able to numb some of the fear of public scrutiny with liquor or coke or weed, depending on my mood and the size of the venue. Clips of me fumbling around on stage still exist on the internet. And while my voice never wavered, it's clear how shit-faced I was.

So much of my young twenties with Visage were spent in a haze, half existing in the present, half six feet under. Even before Lex's death, I wasn't whole, and I have no explanation as to why. No valid reason for the misfires in my brain.

When I'm lurking in those lowest lows, sometimes I'll let myself watch a video or two of Lex performing, lying to myself that they couldn't make me feel any worse. But seeing my brother alive, captured behind that screen, it's always a surprising knife to my chest–his smile brighter than sunlight refracted on the surface of water, his fingers moving so smoothly over the fret of his guitar.

Tonight, I don't have the option of my usual vices to dull the panic and numb the pain from memories. I refuse to let Hail see me that way. So I keep my chin tucked and my hair draped over my eyes as I begin to play without any hesitation. No greeting for this cheering crowd, as usual, though.

They seem confused at first, but when I hit those long, harrowing notes that reverberate through the venue, the crowd falls into my clutches, letting out whistles and cheers.

"Fuck yeah!" some guy screams out, rallying others to join in.

How far do I have to sink before I hit the bottom?

My fury is a boulder, my guilt a knife to cut away each faulty atom

Is there a limit or a measure to this despair?

I suppose I'll keep wading in these murky waters a little bit longer

A little bit longer

Cellphone lights pop up all over the venue as people record, and that twinge of dread returns. If anyone from Visage saw this online, they would recognise my voice instantly. Jackson's warning rings through my head, so much worse than Eric's utter silence when I fled town.

My fingers tremble as I slide them over Liam's fresh guitar strings, but thanks to years of obsessive practice, I don't miss a note.

Why did I agree to this?

Maybe because I hoped I would feel different when I got out here. Because I'm desperate to move forward. To change. To become what Atonement needs.

Really, I think it's because I'd do anything for Hail, even if it means a night of suffering from fallout to allow him the time to warm up properly.

My feelings for Hail go deeper than anything I've ever felt. And with Lex gone, my sick brain wants to latch onto him like a parasite.

My time ends quicker than expected, and I'm left a hollowed shell as I move off the stage with stiff, robotic limbs. Writing songs has always been cathartic, but sharing them with hundreds, no *thousands,* of strangers? A blade to my skin, slicing over and over again.

And the fact that this is the first real show I've put on, at least to an attentive crowd, since Lex's death? One that isn't more interested in Selma's cocktails than what I have to offer on a tiny stage in a dingy, underground bar?

I don't register Hail's words in my ear as he embraces me. Too much blood is whooshing through my head. I barely feel his lips on my jaw. Brushing past him, I shove through the exit door at the back of the venue. He starts after me, but I hear Sondra yelling for him to get his ass on stage.

Cool night air hits my clammy skin. The back door slams behind me, and I'm left alone as I should be, no matter the nagging voice in my head warning me that I should be back inside working. I'm failing Liam.

Immediately, I throw up stomach acid in the alley. How long has it been since I've eaten? I can't even remember. Most of the time, I don't even feel hungry, though I know I should be.

I slump down against the brick exterior, head hung between my bent legs, until Atonement finishes shredding their fans. Hail busts out of the door, panting and high on adrenaline. He's coated in a delicious sheen of sweat, beaming with that megawatt smile of his.

Malek and Griff spill out, followed by Liam, who pops a leg against the building and lights up a blunt.

"That was fucking insane!" Malek exclaims, clapping me on the shoulder. "Oh shit, did you just puke?"

"Isn't the adrenaline great?" Griff beams. "Z, you can never leave us."

Griff orders one of our hired security guards to drive us somewhere in the SUV, rallying everyone's votes in favour of pizza and beer. I remain frozen, crouched on the ground, fingers digging into my scalp, when the SUV pulls up to the curb.

Hail squats down in front of me. He hooks an arm around my neck and pulls my forehead against his chest. "You crushed it. I knew you could do it."

He and Malek haul me up onto my feet and help me into the vehicle, but my skin and bones are too heavy, and their voices are nothing but a warble in my ears. I feel like I'm stuck between dimensions, not fully present in either place. I know for a fact I'm overstimulated, so much so that I can't even voice the fact that I no longer want to be in public. Or process sound. Or feel my body.

We end up at a corner restaurant downtown with an impressive bar. It's packed with young, beautiful people, noise spilling out into the busy streets.

As soon as we enter, I fight to swallow, my throat tightening as my gaze runs over the glittering bottles along the back wall before I even digest the volume of people packed into the tight space.

Our security guy cuts us a direct path to a half-moon booth in the back. I'm the first to scoot in, eager to distance myself from the bar. It shouldn't have come as a surprise that Atonement occasionally ventures out for some fun. They're all still young. They're famous. And they're untethered from responsibility outside of performing.

Hail leans in toward my ear. "Need a Coke or water, sunshine?"

Still feeling disconnected from my body, I have to work overtime to shake my head. Did I leave part of my soul on that stage tonight? Do I need to go collect it? Shouldn't I feel fucking worthless for partaking in the very thing I swore to never do again after Lex's lungs filled with water?

He couldn't fucking breathe. So why do I deserve to?

I keep my eyes anchored to Hail as he strides up to the bar with his bandmates. A group of young people recognise them, aggressively slapping arms and tossing grins their way. Two well-dressed women with tattoo sleeves ask Hail for a picture.

Here I am, tucked in a cheap booth by myself, smelling like a fucking dumpster mixed with vomit, and rapidly spinning down into another destructive mood. And there are the fans, smiles a mile wide and eager to please. Capable of making Hail happy.

They're all bombarded with more pictures and requests for autographs while the bartender fetches drinks. Hail's melting them with his dimpled smile, southern charm at its finest.

This is so fucking wrong. Me being here is *wrong*. I don't belong in his life. I'm not a member of Atonement. With the way things are developing tonight, I don't think I ever could be.

Swallowing down another surge of acid from my stomach, I mentally tally up the distance back to the hotel. We were maybe in the car for fifteen minutes, but it was stop and go traffic.

I slide out of the booth and cut through the tables, head lowered. Liam's eyes are the only ones that catch mine as I slip out, permitting Hail the freedom to choose someone else. Anyone else.

Just not me.

I catch Z pushing through the front doors of the restaurant and rush after him, but out on the streets, he's no more apparent than a ghost. Head whipping around, I seek his tall form out in a mess of vehicles and swarms of drunk, sloppy pedestrians trying to cross the streets.

Fuck.

I want to scream. Instead, I yank out my phone and call him while I cut toward our hotel. My heart pounds faster with every unanswered ring, and dread coils in my gut, pushing my legs to move faster.

When the glass hotel looms before me, I spot him striding with purpose across the parking lot. His hood is drawn low, and his shoulders look like they're caving in on his heart.

"Z," I shout, breaking into a sprint.

I bump shoulders with an employee in the hotel lobby, stumbling to catch my balance as I see Z step into an elevator. His empty gaze locks onto mine before the doors close. Every time I see that look, it feels like staring back into the eyes of death. It chills me to the core.

What the hell is tormenting him? Why won't he let me in? I'm sick and tired of surface-level shit. It's all I've ever gotten from my relationships, not that Z and I are even in one. This is why I gave up on finding someone ages ago.

And yet, here I am. Bounding up the seven flights of stairs to demand Z give us a fair chance. To trust me. To lean on me like a partner. An equal.

Bursting out of the stairwell, I'm just in time to hear a door slam. I run over to Z's door and bash my fist against it. Over and over, I rattle it on its hinges.

When it's clear he's not going to let me in, I resort to begging. "Please, Z. Please don't shut me out. Let me help."

Minutes tick by as my brain plays, "what did I do wrong?" Russian roulette. I'm about to return to the lobby to have a new key made when the lock clicks and he swings the door open.

His expression is vacant, though his body is coiled up like a frightened, wounded animal in the face of a predator. "What do you want from me?"

I throw out my arms. "Are you serious? I don't know, how about an explanation as to why you're spiraling out again?"

So much for begging him to date me.

"None of your fucking business," he mumbles, then goes to shut the door in my face. I catch it, splitting my knuckles on the metal doorframe. Ignoring the blood beading there, I shove my way into his room.

A flash of panic lights up Z's pale, wide eyes as he backs up. We continue this aggressive dance until his ass bumps against his desk.

Nowhere to run now, Z.

"Tell me, does this have anything to do with the reason you quit Visage and disappeared five years ago?"

Not the ideal situation to admit that I know some truths about him, but I can't help the little bit of venom seeping into my tone. Why can't I be aggravated that he's trying to keep me at arm's length? He draws me in enough to give a taste of what we could be, then shoves me away.

His eyes narrow. "You don't know shit about me."

I am not an angry person. I'm not. And that's evident in my lack of ability to control my flailing arms right now. "Other than the fact that you're a phenomenal lyricist and musician, and the captor of my fucking heart, you're right!" I yell. "I don't know shit about you, but I want to. I want us. So bad it fucking keeps me up at night. So bad I ache for it every second of the day."

He seals his eyes shut and shakes his head. "No. You need to quit, Hail. Quit fucking pushing this. I warned you that this thing between us isn't a good idea. You keep dragging me into the uncomfortable."

His words slice through me. Wincing, I step back. "That's how you grow, Z. You volunteered to perform tonight. No one expected you to, though we were all more than happy to let you take the stage."

"I didn't agree to going out afterwards," he mutters, turning his head away. "All I want is some peace and quiet. Maybe for eternity."

My hands ball into fists. "Why didn't you communicate that? No one would have cared if you just wanted to come back to the hotel. Hell, we would have all joined you."

"No one should have to cater to me."

"Who the hell says we're catering, Z?" My voice rises. "We all like you. We want to spend time with you."

A muscle in his jaw spasms, and then his body lowers to the floor. Heart lurching, I sink down with him, pressing my palm against his tear-soaked cheek. "This up and down thing is really fucking with me, sunshine. You're giving me nothing to go off of here."

He closes his eyes, fresh, hot tears spilling over my hand. He releases a defeated breath. "I can't do this."

I withdraw my hand like he's burned me. My nose scrunches as another wave of pain radiates from my cracking heart. "What does that mean?"

In his silence, his answer is crystal clear.

"You can't do this with me," I say softly, fighting back the sting of tears. I've been patient. Well, as patient as I'm capable of being. I was ready and willing to do whatever it took to keep him around. To make him mine.

When he still doesn't answer, I rise up with a sniffle. "Got it. Way to make it loud and clear. I'll leave you to it, then."

Almost every part of me thrashes to stay with him, convinced he needs me to hold him together tonight, but my last bit of self-preservation is telling me to get the fuck out before I fall apart, too; just like I did when I walked in on my ex.

I'll never be good enough, will I?

I leave Z in the dark, just like he asked.

The city looks so much less intimidating from the roof of the hotel. No wonder superheroes have such confidence. From my spot perched on the ledge, I feel like a god watching over tiny humans scurrying below.

But even at this height, you can barely glimpse any stars, and that makes my chest feel a bit hollow. Makes me pine for my parent's sprawling back porch where I'd lay out in a hammock and dream of fame.

That was when I was forced into football and track and AP classes. Then I set off a bomb in our house when I shared the news that I was dropping out of school and quitting all of my activities to join a garage band.

I dangle my legs off the edge as I light up a cigarette from the fresh pack I bought across the street at a shady convenience store. It's a disgusting habit—I even hate the smell on other people—but it's always done the trick to turn the dial down on my anxious energy.

And right now? I'm more than a little keyed up.

The fight with Z was one thing. Obviously, I'm not pleased about it. Still, I'm more worried that he might quit the tour because that's how my brain works. Forget how I feel. I care about Z's well-being more. That's always been my problem, right? I fucking care more.

I mean, I get why people don't want to sign up for long term with me. Once they see past surface level Mykhail Koval, what is there to keep them around? Some goofy smiles and golden retriever loyalty? The persona I take on stage is nothing like how I act in real life, and that always seems to bother people.

No, the icing on the cake to this shit night was the voicemail I got from my sister, Stasi.

Puffing out curls of smoke, I startle as the roof door screeches all the way open. I'd left it propped with a rock so I wouldn't get locked out, though I know Liam would always answer my call to get me out of a bad situation.

"Here I thought I'd have the roof to myself tonight," Liam says, running a hand through his long hair.

I drop my focus back to the streets as he hoists himself up on the ledge next to me and swipes a cigarette. He's never been a smoker other than the occasional joint or blunt. Told me he's not interested in anything that might require commitment. Which means he's smoking to keep me from polishing off the pack.

I watch him blow out a long trail of smoke. "What's going on in that troubled head of yours, Hail?"

My thumb swipes over my palm nervously. "Stasi left me a message. I guess Max had his kid today. No call from him or my parents. No pics sent." I draw more smoke into my lungs, knowing I'll regret this decision tomorrow when my throat aches. "Radio silence fucking sucks, man."

Not to mention I just got shut down by the guy I'm falling for. A guy that doesn't want me. How pathetic am I?

Liam nods and stubs out his cigarette. He lines it up next to the pack. "I get why that could be difficult. They showed you a glimpse of what family should look like, and then they ripped it away when you decided to pursue a dream."

I hang my head lower. "I'm sorry, Liam. I'm not trying to be whiny or ungrateful for what I do have."

Liam hasn't had anyone in such a long time. I still remember attending his dad's funeral. How silent Liam became after. When it was evident his mom wasn't going to show up to finally parent, he was placed with a foster family until he turned eighteen and booked it the hell out of their life soon after.

At least my parents put in effort to start. It was just my choices they didn't agree with that resulted in them cutting ties.

Well, except Stasi. Thank god for my twin.

"Wasn't implying you were either of those things. I just imagine it must be hard for you. With my parents, I knew where I stood from day one. No confusion. No heartbreak." He shrugs.

"God, that's horrible." Tears well in my eyes once more, and I reach for another cigarette. Damn it, why am I so emotional tonight? "Can I dig up your father's corpse and punch him in the teeth?"

Liam gives a hearty chuckle. "I got in enough blows of my own before the fucker croaked."

When I polish off my third cigarette, I circle back to the main reason for my sorry state. "You know I've wanted nothing else but music for the longest time."

"Yeah, I know."

"I should be satisfied with where I'm at, right?" I glance over at him, eager for answers. Desperate for him to point me in the right direction. "Music should be enough."

"Nothing's wrong with wanting a relationship, Hail," Liam replies. "I know I'm not the best person to promote that notion."

I can't help but snort. "You're really not. Have you ever had a girlfriend?"

He shakes his head. "No interest, thanks."

I draw a leg up and cradle it against my chest. "I may have fucked things up tonight. Everyone's hoping Z will fill the hole you're about to punch into the band. But I threw myself out there and pushed him to the edge…"

Liam sighs heavily. "Told you fuckers this old man is tuckered out."

"I know. I get it." I roll my eyes and chuckle.

"It's not up to you to decide for him, Hail. He'll figure out what he needs to do to get to where he wants to be. Might take a few months. Might take years."

I nod and swipe at my stupid runny nose, struggling with the idea of not having Z in my life for that long.

Liam gives my head a little shove. "I envy your heart. You go to bat so hard for everyone you care about."

"And I get left in the dust every time," I mutter. "I envy *you*. Cold-hearted Liam who never falls in love. Protects his heart with a barbed wire electric fence and swooping, man-eating vultures."

"You've been spending too much time around Malek."

I laugh, but it comes out more solemn than intended. "Thanks for listening. I think I'm gonna turn in."

Liam smirks, rare dimples popping up on his cheeks. "You just don't want to cry in front of me."

I tug on the ends of his ridiculously long hair. "I do that too much already."

Strolling back down the stairs, I hesitate at Z's door. Indecision stretches me between our separate rooms. I want to check on him. I want to make things better. Mostly, I want to make sure he's okay.

Knowing I'll be as stiff as a board tomorrow morning, I slide down the wall next to his door and close my eyes.

If I keep lending my heart out as a doormat maybe someday I'll have enough nerve damage like Liam that I won't feel anything anymore.

TWENTY-THREE

Z

"**Z**ander," Lex draws out the sound of my name on a groan. He stumbles after me, lanky body edging the pool on the back patio of whatever random musician's house we're partying at tonight.

Our hidden identities offer us some privacy, but we still play a risky game of joining a wild party or two thrown behind scenes. Musicians assume we're part of the crew or newbies just starting out, eager to make connections with celebrities.

"Z, I don't feel right." Lex clutches his shoulder-length dark hair at the roots. "Something's wrong with my head."

"Yeah, you're high." Scowling at his pathetic form, I brush him off, cutting for the patio doors. "Get some water and get your shit together before you embarrass us all."

My attention refocuses on Jackson, our bassist, smiling coyly at me from the glass sliding doors. He's wearing his black, sleeveless Slayer shirt under a leather jacket and fitted black jeans that make me salivate. His finger curls in a taunt before he spins around and disappears in the clusters of drunk people gathered in the kitchen.

Electric energy crackles under my skin. His intent has been clear from the way he's been eye-fucking me on stage the last few weeks.

As soon as he found out I play hard for the other team, it was game on. We've jammed together for years. How did I miss the signs? We could have been hooking up a hell of a lot sooner.

"Can you just take me home?" Lex whines, grabbing onto my arm. God, the whole bad boy vibe he has on stage is a hoax. Right now, he's nothing more than a baby I didn't ask to take care of. Which is exactly what he is. If the fans knew who they were actually lusting after... He's still underage and has already been exposed to more adult things than I will ever fess up to, all thanks to me.

"Not right now," I growl, breaking away from his hold. "Fucking hell. Lay off the drinks or whatever the fuck you smoked and chill out."

He moans again, curling in half. My features twist in disgust when I think he's about to throw up on my shoes. I give him a little shove, then stalk for the door back into the house.

My brain fires a warning that my little brother isn't well. I promised Mum I would take care of him when I convinced her to let him join the band. In reality, I selfishly only wanted his skill on the guitar. But logic takes a back seat, my body too wired up from the line I snorted in the bathroom a little bit ago and the offer we just received from a big name label.

I didn't come here to babysit. I came here to get my dick sucked and celebrate.

I trail our bassist up the narrow staircase. We make it to the first empty room, and he locks the door behind us. His pierced tongue flicks out over his bottom lip as he drags his gaze up and down my body. "No more distractions."

"None," I agree with a nod.

"The things I'm going to do to you—"

"All of them. *Now*. Get on your knees." I shove him down with a hand on his shoulder and take out my painfully hard dick. His wide eyes flit up to mine, slightly alarmed.

"Sultry voice and you're packing? Shit, you're a treat, Zander."

He draws me into his warm mouth, and I'm dissolving into pleasure. I grip the hair at the top of his head and drive into him. Harder. He gags, but takes it like a good fucking slut, so I pound into him unrestrained, wanting to see tears streaming down his face. Wanting to see just how much of me he can take. Wanting the pressure of that piece of metal along the underside of my dick.

I'm close to nutting down his throat when a knock rattles the door.

A growl rips free. "I swear to god—"

"Zander!" Eric, our drummer, calls out.

"This had better be fucking good," I yell through the door.

"You got eyes on your little brother, dude? He's got me worried. He's pretty fucked up. Told him not to accept anything from strangers."

I slam my head against the door and jam my dick further down Jackson's throat, chasing my release. The knock comes again, and Jackson pops off me. He wipes his mouth on the back of his hand and slides his body up mine as he rises to his feet.

So much for no distractions.

"You think we should check on Lex?" he asks, brows furrowing.

"Damn it!" I rage, stuffing my half hard dick back into my boxers. Without fixing my trousers, I rip open the door and stumble down the hall. "Lex!" I roar, unconcerned about disturbing the party. If Lex is going to stop me from getting off, then I get to be angry.

I storm down the stairs, eyes scanning over too many people crammed into the small house. Music blasts from speakers, vibrating the furniture as I stumble against it. No towering dark-haired figure to be found, I weave my way back to the patio where I last saw my brother.

Worry builds in my gut. Did he leave? Did someone take advantage of him and pull him into a bedroom? If so, I'm getting booked for murder tonight.

I will my limbs faster, quickly zipping up my fly as my heart beats erratically, chugging thick blood through my veins. The patio is still empty, but then I see something lurking at the bottom of the pool.

Invisible hands rip my heart from my chest, snapping arteries and all. *No.* That can't be him.

I throw myself into the deceivingly deep pool head first. Cold water chills my skin as I swim down and wrap an arm around Lex's waist. I haul him to the surface, drawing us over to the edge of the pool.

"Someone call 9-9-9!" I scream over the blaring music.

Eric rushes over, hands grabbing at Lex's shirt and lifting him onto the pavement. I clamber out, dropping to my knees hard enough to split the skin.

Why isn't he spitting out water? Drawing in breath?

The music continues to blast from the house. Jackson sets into motion, barging inside, cursing and shouting for people to turn it off. His eyes keep sweeping back to Lex with feral panic as he raises his phone to his ear and yells into it.

"He's not breathing," I shriek. "Why's he not breathing?"

"Zander." Eric's careful tone shatters me.

Fuck. Fuck. Fuck.

My head darts around the party in desperation. "How did he end up in the pool? Did someone push him in? Who fucking did it?"

No one fesses up, and I know the truth. I left him out here alone, tripping on something he took when I wasn't watching him like I should have been. Left him high and scared and pleading for my help.

Tears spill from my eyes as I slam my hands down on his ribcage, willing the water from his lungs. His lips are blue, his skin too cold. I pry his mouth open and force air into his lungs.

But there's no pulse when I rest my fingers against his neck.

My vision blurs and I let out a sob, collapsing over the corpse of my little brother as sirens wail in the distance and people scatter from the scene like roaches.

TWENTY-FOUR

Hail

I wake up in the hotel hallway, cramped and groaning.

Call me weak, but the idea of getting back on the bus after the way Z and I left things the other night makes my stomach contort.

Will he even be getting on the tour bus?

My fist comes down on his door. When he cracks it open, to my utter shock, his eyes are rimmed with red and his hair is plastered to his head on one side like he slept on a hard surface. He's shirtless and dressed in my favorite low-riding sweats.

At least he changed sometime in the night. That's good, right? Did he sleep at all? Where do we stand now? Can I just fucking hug him already?

"Hey." I push the word out, wincing at the sharp pain in my throat from my idiotic chain-smoking.

"Hey."

I pop my knuckles, struggling to pluck the right words to branch the distance between us. "I'm sorry for last night."

He reaches out to grip my shirt in his fist, then he draws me against his body, tucking this head into the crook of my neck. My breath comes out in a long gust as if I'd been holding it all night.

"I care so much for you. I hope you know that," I say, nuzzling in tighter. "I would never want to force you into a situation you're not comfortable with."

"I know," Z says. "Sorry for the way I acted last night. It was hard getting back out there. Different from Selma's. I thought I could handle it. When I couldn't, I resorted to normal dickish behaviour."

I hold him for a while, basking in his clean scent, my lips brushing over his smooth, addictive skin. Clearing my throat, I dare ask, "So, are we good? I mean, are you quitting the tour or..."

"I'm not quitting." His fingers clench around my shirt tighter. "I'm not giving up on us, either. If that's something you still want with me."

Gently, I take his chin in my hand and lure his mouth to mine. We kiss long enough to toe up to the line of what is publicly acceptable, and then my stomach growls, causing us both to chuckle.

"Well, you know what this calls for?" I ask, nipping at his ear.

"More sex?" His tone is hopeful.

I chuckle. "Breakfast first, tiger."

Z eases back, his brows furrowed. I run my thumb along his sharp jawline, questioning my determination to go out when we could order DoorDash and hole up in a hotel room instead.

"You ever had Snooze before?"

"Snooze?" His brows furrow.

I grin. "Flights of pancakes and big cups of coffee."

Z offers me a soft smile. Chalk that up as a win.

Sitting across from each other in the wacky diner, I order every flavor pancake on the menu. Blueberry danish. Sweet Potato. Strawberry shortcake. You fucking name it. Add in a side of bacon, and two cappuccinos, and perfect, golden sunlight pouring through the windows, and we're both happy campers. It's doing wonders to help me forget how messed up last night became.

"How long have you known?" Z asks, stabbing at the last bite of his blueberry pancake.

"Known what?"

His ice-blue eyes bore into mine. "That I was the vocalist in Visage."

I shrug. "Confidential information."

No way I'm giving up Selma's name. I don't want to give Z any reason to cut her out of his life when he needs every positive relationship he can get.

His mouth turns down. "Did you... know from the start?"

Dropping my grin to make sure he understands how sincere I am, I reply, "No, Z. Not from the start. Trust me, I'm not some crazy person trying to out you or take advantage of the very talented, very private, lead vocalist of Visage. I just thought you were some beautiful stranger pouring out raw emotion for everyone in that bar to ignore."

He chews this over and nods, brushing a lock of hair from his eyes. There goes my pulse again, convincing me he's seconds away from shutting me out. Maybe even bolting out the front door. One step forward, two steps back.

Although, if Z ran, I don't think I'd be able to stop from chasing him to the ends of the world.

After a few silent moments draining our coffee mugs, he gives a shy little grin. "No request for an autograph or a picture. Should I be offended?"

My laugh is light enough to float up to the ceiling. "Tell me that's what you wanted. To be mauled by another fan."

He tilts his head to the side. "I might have been happy to oblige any of your requests." His eyes flick down to my mouth and back up to meet my stare. "Still am."

My heart lurches, pumping scorching blood through my body.

"Yeah? How about I stand front and center in the crowd at your next performance? I won't cheer. I won't even move my body. I'll just stare up at you with *fuck me* eyes."

He leans back. "I did not have fuck me eyes!"

The family at the table beside ours glances over in horror, and Z flushes bright red.

"So sorry," he mumbles.

I snicker. Oh, this was a gloriously wonderful idea.

"You totally did," I counter. "Why do you think I leapt off that stage so fast? Admit it, you were there for me."

Pouting, Z's shoulders drop. "Alright. Maybe I was, but you stared at me first."

"I sure fucking did, sunshine. I sure fucking did."

Z cracks a tiny, mischievous smile, and my heart thuds faster. These little glimpses of happiness from him are a shot of adrenaline to my system.

"Can I tell you another secret since you seem to be so good at keeping them?" he asks.

"Oh, I don't know. Your secrets are such a burden," I tease with a roll of my eyes.

He glances down at his cleaned plate. "Pancakes are my favourite."

My smile breaks wide open. "Fucking nailed it. This must be the best date you've ever been on."

His tiny smile waivers. "It's the only date I've been on."

Honest blue eyes dart up to meet mine, and it takes me a few seconds to process what he just admitted. How can I be both sad and pleased at the same time? I want to be his only, but I also can't believe that no one else chased this beautiful man down.

Reaching a hand over to give his a squeeze, I finally say, "I promise it won't be our last."

Apparently, breakfast is key to stirring up my sex drive. That, or I've missed Hail's touch.

Headed back to our hotel rooms, I shove him against the elevator wall as soon as the doors close on us. I crush my mouth to his, hands roving up under his shirt to trace over each defined, perfect muscle.

He meets my energy, spinning us around until he has me pinned, one hand putting pressure just under my jaw and the other running along my solid length, squeezing me through the fabric of my trousers.

"Careful, Z. Unless you want me taking that fine ass right here," he says, sinking teeth into my earlobe, one of his favourite places on my body to punish. "How many floors do you think you would last before spilling for me?"

I squirm in his hold, thrusting my hips hard into his hand.

"I need you," I murmur.

I needed him last night, even though I drove him away. It's a constant war in my head: selfishly keep him close or protect him by keeping him away. I've proven logic doesn't win out, which is so unfair to Hail. I've hurt him just like I've hurt everyone else in my life.

He presses his mouth to mine. "I know."

The doors part, and a throat clears. My eyes flick to Liam standing there in gym shorts and a sleeveless top. His black waves are damp along his scalp from an intense workout.

Liam steps into the elevator. "Have a good breakfast?"

Hail chuckles as he runs the tip of his nose along my neck. I can't help a little whimper as his palm still works at my straining dick.

The elevator doors shut once more, and I feel Liam's gaze slide over me, watching with molten intensity that heightens the thrill of getting caught. Blood begins to boil in my veins when I see his eyes lower to Hail's hand sliding along my length.

God, what is happening right now?

"You into this, Liam?" Hail's voice is a low, seductive rumble against my skin, causing me to shudder.

Liam fully turns his body toward us, leaning back against the wall and crossing his arms over his broad chest. He continues to watch in silence as Hail flicks open my jeans and slides his hand beneath my boxers. Skin on skin, I groan and push harder into his rough, warm grip.

I know the head of my dick is hanging out. I see Liam staring down at it. He gives nothing away in his expression, but I swear I witness a gleam of something savage in his dark eyes.

The elevator stops and the doors open.

Liam strides out, tossing a quiet, "Not rough enough for me," before disappearing into his room. Hail withdraws his hand, only to hook fingers through my belt loops. He keeps his mouth on mine as we stumble down the hall to his door.

He swipes his key card as we both fight for dominance, heated tongues twirling and hands grasping at hips, ass, dicks. We fumble into his room.

"Bed," he growls.

"Bed," I agree, hauling his shirt off his body. I dip down to suck at his pierced nipples, running my tongue along each bar. I'm in lust with every inch of him. Every inked-over muscle being exercised right now.

Hail lifts me up. I wrap my legs around his waist as he carries me across the room, dropping me onto the bed with caveman aggression. Climbing over me, his hips thrust my body up and up until my head is on the pillows. A soft laugh escapes me.

"Heathen," I whisper, smiling.

"Don't tease me," he chuckles, nipping at my stomach. "You should pity me. I'm in agony every second I don't get to have my hands on you."

"You're ridiculous," I murmur, gently running fingers through his silky hair.

My head drops back onto the pillows as he jerks my unzipped trousers and boxers off and swirls his tongue around the head of my cock.

"So fucking sexy, too. Good with that tongue," I add on a hiss.

He bobs down on my dick until it hits the back of his throat, and I unleash a toe-curling moan. "*Fuck.* Hails."

His hands slide around to knead my ass and then draw my thighs further apart. His tongue runs over my tightening balls, lower and lower, until he's circling my hole, and I'm gripping the comforter in nervous, shaky anticipation.

"You don't need to... *oh, god*!" I gasp as he thrusts his tongue in and out of me a few delicious times.

"Just needed to taste you," he replies darkly, then he reaches for his nightstand, pulling out a bottle of lube.

As he moves a slick hand down my crease, all of my guilt and anxiety from the other night dissolves, and I give into him. Slowly, he pushes a finger inside me, and I forget how to regulate my breathing. When he gets two more in, I'm a trembling mess.

"I need... *fuckkk*... I need..."

He kisses my hip bone. "I know, Z. Now get up here and ride my dick."

With a smooth movement, he flips us over, my heavy dick thudding against his as he places me on his waist. I snatch the lube and stroke a good portion of it down his thick cock. I rock back against it a few times before lining it up with my prepped ass.

"Sit," he orders, hands snapping to my hipbones.

Together, we force my body down and down, taking our time until I'm fully seated. When the burn eases, I start moving, grinding both of us to the edge. He keeps giving me little compliments that have my heart swelling too much in my chest.

You're so good for me. So fucking perfect. So beautiful. All mine, sunshine. You belong to me.

There's too much pressure everywhere. Head tipping back on a moan, I give in and explode, spraying his abs with ropes of warm cum before I can stop it.

Hail grips my ass and thighs and drives his dick up into me, skin slapping against skin. He lets out a low growl as he spills his hot release inside of me, keeping himself buried deep.

I drop my sweaty forehead to his heaving chest.

More. Give me everything, I'm desperate to ask.

I want everything.

I want him. Forever.

And that's the most dangerous thought I can have.

In my dream, I'm laying in my childhood bed. It's pitch-black outside the single window, but I get a sense of something off. Dread heavy in my limbs, I walk to my bedroom door and creep down the hall.

The fear in my gut expands. It's that same feeling when you think someone broke into the house or monsters might actually be real and one is lurking in your closet, waiting to pounce after months of watching you sleep. Cataloguing you like a fucking serial killer.

I haven't spent much time in this house since Visage started touring. It's not a place that feels like home, but I don't really know what else to do with myself. I don't feel like a real person. Not since...

Lex.

Tears prickle my eyes, but my body won't allow me to cry. It's a cruel form of punishment, allowing these horrible emotions to bubble up inside me with no possibility of release.

Shuffling down the stairs, my feet step on something wet. It's too dark to see, but maybe Mum splashed water on her way up to bed. She does that sometimes. Realises how drunk she is and tries to down a bunch of water to minimise the damage the next morning.

She used to make us pancakes, too, as an apology. *Sorry I fucked up and hit the bottle again. But do you remember when your dad did this funny thing? Do you remember his laugh? You know why he left us, right? You know this is your fault, Zander. It's your fault I have to drink.*

I used to believe if I hid her bottles or drained them in the sink that she'd have to quit. But the thing about addicts is they'll prioritise their crutch over everything else. The first time I dumped her bottle of whiskey, there was nothing but crackers to eat in the house for three days. I gave most of them to Lex.

Aching for a drink myself or a line to snort, I climb down more steps and enter the small living space. My heart chugs with panicked beats as I back against the wall. There's a body-like figure on the floor, splayed out between the coffee table and the couch.

Someone *did* break in. And I think... *fuck, I think they might be dead.*

I step forward and my feet hit something wet again. Grimacing, I flick on the light. Not water. *No.*

I stumble back as I glimpse all the blood on the carpet. The trail of it leading to the body with slit wrists. The body that is my mother.

I switch the light back off, and wake to find myself still trapped in hell.

The incessant buzz of my cell on the nightstand pulls me from sleep.

Bloody fucking hell. If Hail keeps up this early morning shit, I'm going to have to find a way to become a morning person, so I don't snap at him. These memories that keep popping up in my sleep and waking me in a panic aren't helping.

Rolling over in Hail's hotel bed, I grab my phone and open it up to his message of heart emojis and a selfie of him on a walk through downtown, hair tied up and grinning in such a precious way, my chest constricts painfully.

But then my sleepy eyes adjust to the eighteen new missed calls from unknown numbers. Horror unfurling in my gut, I listen to the first voicemail and my heart drops out of my chest. Detached from reality, I watch it beat on the floor while I clutch the phone to my ear.

"Zander Graves? This is Elevated Rock Magazine. We'd love to feature an article about you in our next issue if you're interested. Please gives us a call—"

Next voicemail. Same thing.

"Zander, this is Bella Rodriguez from Spinhaven Records reaching out to see if you have time to meet with us. We're huge fans of Visage—"

Blood whooshes in my ears. What the fuck is happening?

My stupid brain wonders if I made a mistake letting Atonement into my life. Could they have dropped my identity to someone? Did Hail tell someone? Did Selma? Would she betray me like that?

I stumble out of bed and cross the hall between our rooms. Tucked in the privacy of my own room, I retrieve my laptop with shaking hands. Google reveals dozens of recent articles about my revealed identity as the lead singer for Visage, as well as the other members of the band.

A sickness blooms inside of me. There's more in-depth knowledge about my life than I've ever shared. Raw details on my drug and alcohol use. My apparent temper. *My brother had just fucking died and my mother was spiraling down into a bottle, you asshats.*

To add to the churning bile in my stomach, there are even a few rumors about my ties to Hail. *Metal God Intimate with Trouble-Making Zander Graves?*

Sure enough, someone posted fucking pictures of us holding hands in that cafe when we first met. It's like the whole world is standing before a bulletin board of my life, pinning strings together to figure me out for no good reason other than to prove what a piece of literal garbage I am.

There are comments praying for my return to music, but for every one of those, there are two more to cut me down.

Hopefully, he doesn't join Atonement and wreck them, too. Go back to being nobody, Zander.

Fucker is a drug addict. No wonder he could write good songs. I could do the same thing blitz out of my mind.

I swear to god he pushed his brother into that pool. My cousin was at that party. Zander was an absolute dickhole.

Yeah, those ones fucking suck. But it's the rumors about Hail that trouble me the most.

I don't think I can listen to Mykhail anymore without thinking about him taking dick up the ass.

Great, he caught the Zander disease. Enjoy the descent into hell, Hail!

And then there are the pictures of my brother.

I'm shaking. The media has no fucking right to share this information with the public just for entertainment purposes. Don't they realise we're fucking humans? That we're entitled to some privacy, too? I suppose all respect for that goes out the window when you achieve a bit of fame.

My stomach churns. God, there are even pictures of Lex and me as kids, dressed in superhero pjs and camping in the backyard. Pictures only my mother would have had.

White-hot betrayal stabs at my aching, fragile heart. Did she... did she sell me out to the media? A final 'fuck you' for taking everything from her? Is this about quid?

Of course it's about quid. That's all she's ever fucking cared about.

I drop my head between my knees, holding back the urge to puke all over the patterned carpet. Is there anywhere I could go that they wouldn't follow me? Any way I can salvage Hail's reputation before I butcher that, too?

I tug at my hair. I don't want to do this again. My chest is heaving. My lungs are convinced there's not enough room in this stuffy, dark hotel room to satisfy my body's needs.

Needs. What do I need?

My eyes flit to the minibar, and for the first time in five years, I swipe a bottle of liquor, getting to work numbing reopened wounds.

My relapse into multiple bottles isn't what does me in, unraveling five years of lying low and avoiding my addictions.

I can recover from the drinking. I can. I know this for a fact because the minibar in my room is now empty and, after a run to the corner shop across the street, my bank account is, too.

Thank god I didn't have to answer to Hail on why I reek of a concoction of liquor. He and the Atonement boys are out doing a radio interview.

So I fight to pull myself back together.

After taking a long shower in which I ran the water hot enough to turn my body red, and scrubbed my raw skin three times, I dress in all black and pull up my hood. I set out with guitar and notebook in hand, needing a change of environment and my music to figure out my shit before I do a whirlwind dive so far down there will be no hope of recovery.

I can bounce back from this.

But when I reach the hotel lobby, I'm met with a ghost from my past. Blood drains from my body as I spot Jackson sprawled in a lobby chair facing the elevators. Sitting there like he's been waiting for me. Which is exactly what he's been doing.

Did the media leak my current location, too?

Jackson's chestnut hair is cropped short to his head now, and the hard edge to his features is out of place with the easy-going guy I knew when we played music together. Guilt jabs at me, and I tuck my head, striding for the doors. My headache throbs with each quick stride I take.

Why did I have to binge on alcohol? Why couldn't I have walked my ass to a store to buy a pack of cigs last night and spared this awful hangover?

"Zander Graves!" his voice slices through me.

Why can't he just keep me in the past? Oh yeah, probably because I fucked them all over. I let one of them drown and then bailed on the others right when we were handed a contract to skyrocket us into fame.

Hands ball up in my hoodie as he stops me in my tracks. "You are a fucking prick!"

He shoves me back, and I don't even have time to brace for the fist that slams into my jaw. My notepad and guitar go flying. I hear the gutting sound of splitting wood on the hard floor, the last of my cherished belongings shattered.

Outrage erupts from guests in the lobby. Someone shouts to the front desk employees to call the police, but no one actually steps in to stop Jackson from dishing out the punishment he obviously stored up for five long years, and I'm too sluggish from booze to move out of his reach or fight back.

Even if I was sober, I wouldn't fight back.

His fist cracks against my cheekbone. Adrenaline running high, I barely feel anything beyond a dull pounding where he landed the punch.

"Where the fuck do you get off on running away like that?" He spits out. "You ruined us, Zander! We had a contract in hand, and you ruined everything! Was it fucking cocaine that night, too?"

Another strike to my jaw. I stumble back and tuck my hands in my hoodie pocket, basking in the promise of pain I'll feel when this is all over.

"Fight back, Zander!" he screams at me. "Why won't you fight back?"

Because I'm fucking dead inside. Because I don't care. Because I deserve this. Go ahead and wreck me. It can't be any worse than what I've already done to myself.

"Hey!" another male voice roars through the hotel lobby.

No. I duck my head as if that will hide my tall frame from Hail cutting toward us, his features twisted in rage.

He steps between us, shielding me. He throws Jackson a, "what the hell, dude?" Then he faces me, wrapping an arm loosely around my head and drawing me close enough to rest his forehead against mine. I wince, certain he can smell the alcohol on my breath. Shame burns in my chest.

"You good, Z? Or you need me to fuck him up? Honestly, I'm not a great fighter, but I'll do my best to make him regret his decision to mess with you."

I shake my head and pull out of his hold. Moving back into my sightline, Jackson points a finger at me. "You should stay away from that one. He doesn't give a shit about anyone but himself. He was too busy getting high and shoving his dick down my throat to give a fuck about his own dying brother."

Hail's wide eyes fall back to me, full of questions. I slip around him and plant myself right in front of Jackson, driven by the need for more pain. I want him to be the vessel for justice. For failing Visage. For letting Lex die. For my mum's depression. For dad disowning us.

"Yeah? Don't act like you weren't too busy sucking it to care about Lex either," I snap back.

It's the wrong thing to say. But again, I'm out of alcohol, and I have limited means to acquire more. My emergency credit card itches in my back pocket, but it's got a pretty low credit limit. One I shouldn't test with temporary means to feel numb.

So what else am I supposed to do to erase this horrible, clawing feeling in my chest other than to entice Jackson to unleash his pent-up hatred?

He hits me again. I go down hard, my head cracking against the floor. Vision blurring, I spit blood and contemplate getting back up.

More, my body urges.

Liam puts an end to my plans. His massive body steps into view, slightly spinning with the room as he squares up to Jackson. "Get the fuck out of here before I break you beyond repair."

Jackson bares his teeth but sizes Liam up and recognises defeat. This doesn't stop him from spitting at my shoes before he leaves. "Whatever. You're not worth the trouble, anyway."

I want to argue that obviously I was if he put in the effort to hunt me down. Instead, I close my eyes and let out a heavy breath. Can I sink into the floor? Dissolve into the little flecks of gold in the marble pattern?

Jackson confirmed my every fear. My absence and Lex's death tanked the band. How many more lives can I ruin before it's enough?

Hail peels me off the floor, but then I'm screaming at him to quit touching me. "Just leave me the fuck alone!"

Startled, he releases his hold, and I stumble for the front doors, not giving a shit about where I'm going, only that I need to be gone.

My own flesh and blood. I let him die. One selfish decision cost me the only person who has ever cared about me. The only person who recognised my existence. Who reminded me I matter when the people that made me would have preferred I'd not been born at all.

Not true. Hail cares. Atonement cares.

The dark shadow in my mind surfaces. *Yeah, but you're doomed to fail them, too.*

The ground lurches beneath me. Only part of my brain registers falling. One heavy blink, I'm looking at the world normally, and the next, it's sideways. Cold water splashes up at my face. Am I lying on the street?

Cars blare their horns and swerve to miss me. I push my head further into the dirty pot hole of rainwater I've found myself in, head spinning and blood running from a cut on my forehead.

I know I should get up, but honestly I'm curious which will kill me first, a car or the rising water. It covers my mouth and nose. I can't breathe, but that's okay. Lex couldn't breathe, either. I wish I could give him the air from my lungs. The worthless beating heart in my chest.

Why did you leave me? Why can't I hear you in my head anymore? Take me with you, Lex. Please, just fucking take me.

Sobs threaten to break free from my chest, and it's all over. I'm forcing my head further down into that water. Drowning in the absolute depths of this guilt. I hear my mum's bitter voice tearing into me.

You did this! You tore this family apart! I told you not to get involved in this lifestyle! I told you to keep your baby brother away from it!

I hear my father's moan of pain on the other end of the phone when he's informed of Lex's death. *Why him? Why couldn't it have been Zander?*

The questions I wasn't supposed to overhear echo in my head, breaking my heart over and over again. *Why indeed, Dad?*

God, isn't grieving supposed to be cathartic? Why does my body feel like it's being ripped in two by invisible hands?

Strong arms pull me off the street. I spit up dirty water. Hack it out of my lungs. Blood immediately drips into my eyes as Liam hoists me up against his solid chest like a child. Why did he follow me?

I writhe against him and plead, "Please don't take me back to Hail. He can't see me like this."

Liam's hold is like an iron vise. He carries me to his Pantera in the parking lot of the hotel. After buckling me into the passenger seat and leaning the seat back, he grabs a folded towel from his gym bag and presses it against the cut above my brow.

"Try not to bleed on my seats," he mumbles, and then he's gunning it through traffic.

Reckless maneuvers take us to the nearest urgent care. Liam sits with me in silence as the doctor stitches my brow back up and gives protocol for a concussion. Then Liam takes me back to his hotel room and props me up in a chair so I won't be tempted to sleep, though the urge to drink or snort something or pop a pill is still fighting for control.

He drops a bottle of water on the table next to me. "I can smell the liquor on you. Do you make a habit out of drinking that much?"

I wince. "No. Not in years."

Liam sits down in the chair opposite me like I'm in an interview with an intimidating CFO.

"You try to kill yourself out there?" His tone is hard, his eyes narrowed. And I recognise it as concern, not anger. Liam is concerned about me.

My chin lowers, my gaze dropping to my fingers picking at the chipping black polish Hail painted on my nails.

"I'm not trying to make you feel a certain way. Just trying to get some answers," Liam explains.

I swallow. "I don't know. Maybe."

"Someone hurt you? That guy in the lobby?" Liam asks, leaning in closer. The sleeves over his biceps lift up enough for me to catch the word *Agony* inked into his skin above something that looks like a demon.

I shake my head. *No, I'm the wielder of all pain.*

"You witness something you shouldn't?" he tries again.

"My brother drowned." I lick my lips and force the words from my mouth. "He was already dead when I found him. He was... messed up, and I left him alone."

Liam sighs and runs a hand over the stubble along his jawline. "Did you ask him to take those drugs?"

My chest is heaving with effort to draw in enough air. "No, but he was just a kid. He needed a better role model than me."

Liam nods. He's glorious to admire, I'll admit, but I practically feel the permafrost at his core. There's something faulty with Liam, just as much as there is with me. A darkness that knows no limits.

"I watched my father drink himself to death," Liam begins slowly. "He couldn't cope with life, and beating the shit out of me day in and day out didn't make him feel any better."

My eyes flit back up to meet his. *Fucking hell.*

Liam breaks our stare first, tugging a business card from his wallet. He slides it across the table. "I've got a professional therapist I talk to on the regular. As much as I fought it for years, she really did help."

My throat tightens as I stare down at the card. I've avoided therapy, partially because I didn't want this pain to be gone. I didn't want to feel happy, but mainly because speaking about Lex's death would give it more finality in my brain.

"Hail would be devastated by the amount of shit you pulled today. Do you understand?" Liam asks, his tone firm.

Ah, there it is. Liam's loyalty to Hail is admirable. And here I am, a threat to Hail's happiness.

Unable to produce sound, I simply nod.

"Promise me you'll give her a call. Promise me, or I cannot sign off on this thing you have with Hail. I cannot allow you to remain here with us."

I know on some level Liam does care about me, but that's not what my brain hears. *Agree to therapy or you're fired.*

"Okay," I whisper, picking up the card.

I'll do him one better and save everyone the trouble.

This time I'll disappear for good.

TWENTY-SEVEN

Hail

Getting held up by the cops is just about the worst thing to happen in my life. I've never been one to disrespect authority—metalheads are actually pretty big sweethearts—but after disclosing about the assault on Z, I verbalize my need to give chase.

Okay, so a couple of "do your fucking jobs" were thrown out there, accompanied by some shoving, which resulted in warnings about handcuffs and a night in jail.

Not my proudest moment. But Z's alone and hurting. I know he doesn't want me. That doesn't mean I'm going to give up on him.

After assuring the guy who attacked Z is taken away in cuffs, Liam and I split up, combing the streets outside the hotel. I wind up drifting about two miles south before I decide to cut back and try another route. He couldn't have gone far on foot.

After an hour of what feels like aimless wandering, I head back to the hotel. I pace between the lobby and Z's door when a text comes through from Liam. *He's in my room safe. I'm headed out to pick up some dinner.*

My feet can't carry me up the stairs fast enough as I fire off a response. *Why didn't you call me sooner?*

Another text pings, a word of caution from Liam. *You know it's not on you to fix him, Hail.*

I scoff. That's like being told to stop loving someone. It's not a switch you can just fucking shut off automatically.

Love.

Is that what this has transformed into? I mean, I know for certain I've always sought out approval from others because I don't have it from the ones meant to love me the most.

I bang on Liam's door, my heart thundering painfully in my constricted chest. Slamming both fists against the surface, I holler for Z to open the door. Locks click from behind me. I turn to glare at the suited man that peeks his head out.

"Bro, can you not?" he asks, glaring right back.

"No!" I rage. "So fuck. Straight. Off."

His brows shoot up, and he quickly slams his door shut, adding to the shitstorm of noise happening in the hall. *Go ahead and call the cops. They've already got my name.*

Unfortunately, the room Z's in is booked under Liam's name, so guest services won't issue me another key. Why didn't he deliver him to a room I have access to? Keep him in the lobby? *Why, Liam? Why torture me like this?*

Liam appears in the hall carrying three boxes of pizza and a sack with 2-liters of Coke. For the first time since I discovered the bruises he hid under his shirt in the fourth grade, back when he was too small to defend himself, I glimpse a flash of fear in his eyes.

He hands me the room key. Slamming the door wide open, I sweep into the room like a bloodhound on a moonlit trail. Dread presses my lungs out and out until my ribs ache. The pressure keeps me from drawing in a full breath.

No sign of Z anywhere. No indication that he was here. That he ever existed.

I whirl on Liam, fists clenched.

"He was here, I swear it," Liam says, shaking his head in confusion. "I wouldn't lie to you, Hail."

"You would if you thought you were protecting me," I exclaim.

Malek peeks his head in the door Liam has propped open with his foot. "What's with all the commotion?"

By this time, I'm seeing red, and the only outlet for this fury is the two people standing before me. I don't even recognize them at this point.

"You should have fucking called me earlier. Why did it take you so long? You said something to him, didn't you? I swear to god, if I find out you fired him, I'm fucking done. I don't even want to do this shit anymore. I'm so fucking sick of this tour. This band. Everything."

I scream out every horrible emotion breaking against my heart like waves against an eroding cliffside.

"What is this about?" Malek's voice is weak, his eyes nearly bugging out of his head.

"Might want to stay out of this one," Liam replies calmly.

My shoulders drop heavy in their sockets. Completely deflated, I sink to the floor and hide my face in my hands.

"Hail." Liam tosses the food and drinks on the table. He sits down behind me and pulls me against his chest. His arms wrapped around me become my anchor.

Tears spill from my eyes, splattering on his forearms covered in tattoos of geometric angels suffering. My angel is suffering right now, and I don't know how to make it stop. I can't shake the image of sorrow etched into his face as that piece of shit tore him apart in the lobby. I can't forget the stench of whiskey on his breath. The disclosure of his brother's death. The crunch of his splintered guitar under my boots.

"I don't know what to do. I just want to be with him. How do I bring him back? How do I save him, Liam?"

"The only one that knows the answer to that is Z," Liam murmurs, tightening his hold on me.

Malek sits down in front of me cross-legged and just rests his hands on my knees, further grounding me.

"Any idea where he could have run off to?" Malek asks.

I shake my head frantically. "None. Absolutely fucking none. He barely told me anything."

"Just breathe, Hail," Liam instructs. "Just breathe."

I curl up into a ball and cry while Liam holds me together, just like I used to do for him. And when my body is a dried up husk, Liam picks up his phone to start making calls. With Malek's steady gaze on me, I spill every guilty, depressing, selfish thought I've had over the last few months.

All the while, I'm convinced I could die from a broken heart.

TWENTY-EIGHT

Z

I make it on the overnight flight to Dublin.

My original goal was to fly into Heathrow and pick up where I left off. I'd grovel to my landlord to get my house back. I know for a fact I wouldn't be accepted in my childhood home, even though I've kept the lights on there for the last five years.

Then I'd meet up with Selma and beg to have a few nights a month performing on her stage. Though I know it's probably hopeless. Even if she was open to talking to me, I don't know that I'm in the right state to ever perform again.

But when I walk up to the line to purchase a plane ticket, I overhear someone's phone blasting some news video.

A fight broke out at the Wyndham Hotel in Oklahoma City yesterday. Members of two separate bands, Visage and the notorious Atonement, clashed with swinging fists, lead vocalist Zander Graves at the centre of it. Spectators recount how the band member identified as Mykhail Koval nearly got himself arrested for assaulting police officers.

With Atonement's recent outburst and rumors stirring about lead guitarist Liam Beckner's decision to exit the band at the end of their U.S. tour, is this the downfall for the Texan metal band?

It's everything I feared. No matter what the truth is, the media and the internet will spin this however they please for more attention.

My fingers tremble and my skin grows clammy, the lack of proper air conditioning in the airport a crime. In my panic, I can't fathom why I'd want to return to a life I hated in the first place. I'm so tired. Tired of surviving. Exhausted by the idea of a future without Atonement. Without Hail's warmth and Liam's encouragement and Malek's teasing and Griff's kindness.

I fell in love with more than one heart on tour.

"Sir?" the man at the counter calls out, gaze circuiting over my cut and bruised face with concern.

Brain firing on very few cylinders, I step up to the counter and ask him to book me on the next flight to Europe using my emergency credit card. Doesn't matter where I end up.

Is there a reason for my existence? Did God decide there were too many pure souls in his world and he needed someone like me to balance them out? Or maybe he just took less time on me.

Because the truth is, I was broken from the beginning. Rewind before Mum's suicide attempt and her drinking and Lex's untimely death. Before sperm donor walked out of our lives. Before years of being shuffled behind Lex, hidden like a stain on expensive furniture.

I was born a half, not a whole.

The moment the plane touches down at the Dublin Airport, I charge two bottles of whiskey to the same credit card. Then I book a hotel room downtown with no intention of coming out.

The guest services employee tries and fails to make light conversation with me as my heart hammers away in my chest, glass bottles heavy in my backpack, and I hope she won't be the one to find me tomorrow.

Partially through bottle number one, I'm laid out on the cold bathroom tile of my room, pissed at myself for taking such a simple way out. Drinking was always easy for me. Would a handful of antidepressants be enough to stop my heart? Would it be more painful?

I'm pissed I didn't get that painkiller prescription filled after my urgent care visit.

Silent tears track down my cheeks as I stare up at the water-stained ceiling. I don't cry for myself. I cry for everyone I've hurt. I know I'm hurting Hail right now, but it's better this way. The tour will keep him distracted, and in time, he'll move on with his life. He'll find a better partner. Someone suited to match the purity of his soul.

God, I'm so stupid for getting involved, but I foolishly trusted myself not to make strong connections. If I hadn't gotten on that stage that night, maybe I would still be working with the crew and creating music with Hail and pretending like everything would work itself out in time.

Fuck me for trying, right?

I press fists against my eyelids, hating my brain for being so messed up. There's really no fixing it. I tuck a hand into my pocket and run fingertips over the edges of the business card Liam gave me.

Biting down on the inside of my cheek, I reach for the second bottle of whiskey instead as the bathroom spins like a merry-go-round. I black out after three more long, burning gulps.

To my disappointment, I wake hours later in a puddle of tears and vomit. *Damn it*. I can't even properly drink myself to death.

I glimpse my phone hanging off the bathroom counter and reach for it to check the time and date. My blood nearly halts in my veins at the volume of missed calls and texts, some from every member of Atonement, Cora and Sondra, too, who I thought only tolerated me because Hail demanded it and I was a decent guitar tech.

I know it's wrong to ignore them. I promised I wouldn't do this again. But the physical act of typing out a response drains me of my last will to live.

I don't want to exist anymore.

Twenty-Nine

Hail

"Hail, you have to get out there. You're on in five," Sondra orders. She keeps her distance, and a spark of guilt hits me because she recognizes how messed up I've been. I emphasize that point as my fist slams into the side of the tour bus hard enough to break skin. I get that pain won't bring him back, but at least it's a reminder of reality.

I've never been an aggressive person, no matter what the fans believe when I fill up that stage with carnal rage. Normally, I bottle up all of my frustrations and leave it out there for the fans, so by the time the show's over, there's nothing angry left tumbling around inside of me.

But it's our first show since Z vanished off the face of the fucking planet, and his absence is noticed by everyone. The crew has been graveyard silent between shows outside of their normal meetings. Z hasn't answered any of our calls or texts. And while I've been tempted to search for family members online, I don't think he has much of a relationship with them from the hints he's given me.

Hell, if I went missing, not only would my parents not know where I ended up, but they probably wouldn't care. I can hear my dad bitching about the effort of having to peel me out of some back-alley dumpster.

With all the fucking outcries the media is making about us right now, they can't seem to put their little detective brains together to help us locate Z.

Shaking my throbbing hand with a curse, I catch Liam staring at me from my peripheral. Malek and Griff are already backstage. Both of them have found it difficult to hold a conversation with me, evident in their awkward, stifled body language.

Both are secretly heartbroken, I think. I mean, how else are they supposed to take it when I admit to not feeling the magic on this tour? Not like I have when Z and I create music.

Jesus, why did everything have to go wrong? What was the tipping point? Was it my efforts to make Z feel loved? Or was it his stress performing on stage again? Would it have been right for me to talk him down from facing his fears? I knew he had them, but I didn't understand the depth of them at that time. I glimpsed the tip of an iceberg that stretched well beneath the surface.

It scares the living daylights out of me that things will never return to normal. And I may never know what happened to him. Whether he's alive or...

Tears burn my eyes as I stroll to the back of the stage, and I squeeze them shut to keep from bawling. *Mykhail Koval caught crying like a baby on stage for his missing gay lover.*

Yeah, I'd probably go on a rampage if the media printed something like that.

"You gonna tend to that hand before we go on stage?" Griff asks hesitantly, pointing his drumstick at the blood dripping from my fingertips.

"Fuck off," I mutter, stalking toward the stage where thousands of chanting fans await.

Liam catches my arm before I make it to the microphone. He pops the cork off a bottle of half-drank vodka and dumps it on my cuts. Then he hands the bottle to the stage crew, proceeding to wrap my knuckles with a strip of his shirt he rips from the hemline.

Clenching and unclenching my wrapped fist, I step up to the microphone. Most shows it takes me a song or two to dig into the level of rage I need to really sell my performance. Today, I'm in hell the moment I open my mouth and unleash the deepest sound my body has ever produced. I want to drag them all down with me. I want them to stand before the devil and receive judgment.

The crowd goes ballistic. Mosh pits open up like whirlpools. Walls of bodies crash together and recede. I'm sure I look fucking feral. Sleepless, drenched in sweat, and still oozing blood from split knuckles.

Everyone who paid to be here will witness the birth of monsters within me, and if they don't survive them, I don't really care.

Without Z, I don't care.

I make it to our second to last song and decide that I'm done. I would give all of this up, the only thing that has brought me joy in this life. All just to wrap my arms around him one more time and tell him that I love him.

To be worshiped by millions of people means nothing if I can't be loved unconditionally by the one person I care about the most.

Removing my guitar, I start to walk offstage. Griff lifts his sticks in question, but I shake my head. *No more.*

"Finish it," I tell Malek, knowing he can carry them through. He's always had the talent.

I pause for a moment to turn and watch Malek step up to the mic. Someone in the crowd screams out in excitement, and then everyone's going nuts as he unleashes the war cries of demons upon them.

Handing off my guitar to a solemn Cora, I keep walking until I'm in the middle of a field right off the highway, the chugging sounds of Atonement fading behind me. That's where I fall apart all over again. Wholly and completely. I don't think there's anything strong enough to mend the shredded muscle in my chest.

Why am I like this? Why do I crave love from those fated to wreck me? Can I blame my parents? Or is it just the way I was put together at an atomic level? Does Stasi feel these bullet holes inside of her, too? Torn flesh and muscle from the verbal insults we were delivered in rapid fire as children when we fell short of expectation. Short of perfection.

Liam wore his wounds on the outside. Bruises. Burns. Cuts. Mine were always internal, hidden behind a perfect, upper class smile.

Those wounds ache for Z now. For the demons he harbored. Why couldn't he trust me to help?

Some time into my misery, ringed fingers gently slide into my hair and tip my head up. Liam hovers over me, blotting out the sun. His bronze skin is tinged red with a sunburn and his long hair is soaked from dumping water over his head.

"I can't watch you fall apart anymore," Liam says, pain etched into his features. "He's in Ireland. Sligo, to be exact."

My eyes grow wide. "How do you know?"

"I hired a private investigator. I was worried for both of you. My PI found record of a plane ticket to Dublin. He stayed there for a night, then checked into a bed-and-breakfast in Sligo." Liam drops his hand from my hair and sighs. "Sondra asked me to stay quiet about it until after the tour, but neither of us likes where this is headed, Hail."

My body sags into the grass, both relieved there's still record of him and also confused at why he would be in Ireland.

What's there for you, Z?

"We'll deal with shit here. Go find him." Liam holds out his cherished car keys. "I'll send you info on his location. You better fucking text me when you land."

I'm nodding my head so hard my brain rattles in my skull. "Okay. Yeah. Okay, you got it."

Before I bolt for the parking lot, I haul Liam into a crushing embrace. "Love you, bro. I don't tell you enough how good you are to all of us."

"Yeah, well, I'm a dick to the rest of the world, so it balances out."

I stare at the waves, my body scraped out on the inside.

All the medication I've tried pumping into my deficient brain, I think, has finally worked itself out of my system. Strangely, my head is clear. I'd probably feel okay if not for the sluggish feeling in my stomach from the amount of liquor I consumed two days ago.

My meager belongings remain at the bed-and-breakfast with the matronly owner. She's been exceptionally kind to me, wishing me a good adventure when I left this morning and promising to have lunch ready by the time I return.

She didn't realise that when I consumed the massive breakfast she prepared, I was savouring my last meal.

At least, that's what I thought at the time. My determination keeps flagging between acceptance and fear like a broken gas gauge when I hear how hard the waves are crashing against the cliff side.

Stripping down to my boxers, my brain is still half-convinced that I'm just going for a swim. And maybe I am.

I climb down the zig-zagging stone steps into a little cove where the ocean isn't so tumultuous. Still fucking stupid to get in, but I didn't come here with the intent of keeping myself safe.

Hesitation creeps in as I close my eyes and picture Hail. His brilliant smile and whiskey-toned eyes. A beautiful angel with a little cross chain dangling from his ear, matching the one I run my fingers over.

I lower myself down a metal ladder off a concrete dock. I cling to it as freezing Atlantic water laps at my waist. The strong push and pull of the water draws me further in until my feet touch rocks at the bottom.

Then I'm swimming away from the dock, out to where I can't touch. Plunging in fully, my thoughts turn desperate, fighting to give me hope, only for it to slip through my fingers moments after. Telling me *hey, maybe today's not the day*. Then setting off alarms that we are at maximum capacity for life. Engines are failing and we're losing oxygen.

Another wave rolls over me, and my head bobs along the surface, my stitched up brow burning from the saltwater. Maybe I'll just tread water for a bit…

I hear my name screamed out. Turning in the water, I glimpse the dock a hundred feet away and a figure standing atop the stairs, waving their arms madly.

Am I hallucinating? Did I stay under the water longer than I thought? Because that's Hail tearing down the steps. *My Hail.*

He's really fucking here. How and why is he here? He should be on tour.

Fear and pain and happiness all latch onto me at once. Hail doesn't hesitate to dive into the water, shoes and all. He's swimming out to me like he's striving for a gold medal. God, why is he swimming like he means it? And the horror that's etched into his face–I think I've shaken hands with that eldritch monster before.

What am I doing?

With tremendous effort, Hail drags me back to the dock and heaves me up onto the concrete. Teeth chattering and body trembling, I sit up to meet his frightened eyes.

And then, oh god, he's sobbing. Fucking crumbling before me, shoulders and chest heaving uncontrollably. I think I see pieces of him breaking off before me. My shaking hands lift as if I can catch them and patch him back together.

Fuck. *Fuck.*

I do the only thing I can think of and wrap my arms around him. I put these fucking cracks in his solid foundation. I am responsible for slowly breaking this man, just like I've destroyed so many others.

Burying my head in his neck, I whisper against his cold, damp skin, "I'm sorry. So, so sorry, baby."

He can barely get words out between gasping breaths. "You. Cannot. Do. This. To. Me."

"I won't. Never again. I'm so fucking sorry." I squeeze him tighter and kiss his shoulder.

I mean it this time. There *has* to be an end to this.

After Hail cries out everything inside of him, I pull him against my chest and rock him for a while. Eventually, he pushes me back until I'm splayed out on the dock. He perches on my hips, pinning me to the hard ground, his hands pressing down on my chest.

I brace. I expect him to yell. Slap me. Shed more tears. Do any and all of the things. Instead, he stays frozen atop me, staring into my eyes as if he wants to paint me to his memory.

"I'm sorry for running, Hails," I murmur, my throat constricting. Fresh, itchy tears spring to my eyes. "I'm not well. Obviously. But you already knew that."

His brows knead together, but still he waits for me to continue. I think he needs this from me. My words. My truths.

"It's just... shameful. So fucking unforgivable what I did to my brother. How I acted years ago."

He doesn't try to argue or persuade me away from what I'm feeling. He just gives me space to feel. When his hands slowly ease down my bare stomach, I lean up to capture his mouth in a deep, endless kiss.

Hunger awakens in me, given a taste of one of my many addictions. Our kisses become frantic. Ravenous. Desperate. He teases me open with gentle nips, tasting me as his tongue sweeps over mine and brushes my bottom lip.

"I'm here for you." Hail maps the words down my jaw and neck. "Whatever you need. Lean on me. Use me. *Love me.*"

All I can do is nod because my desire for him needs to be satisfied. I'm a thief, and he is the precious gem that's caught my eye. He is the rope tossed into the pit I've been dwelling in for five long years, maybe longer.

I need to fucking escape.

I drag his wet clothes off his body. My fingers spread over his beautiful skin, eager to touch as much of him as possible. Cradling a hand behind his head, I roll us over until I'm on top of him.

Leaning down, I lick and suck at his nipples, salty from the ocean. I work my mouth down his shapely abs. Then I'm yanking his trousers off and taking his cock into my mouth, eager to please him.

Two hands dive into my hair, gripping at the roots. "Fuck. You are so good. I need you to understand how good you are, sunshine."

Hips jerking, his dick hits the back of my throat. I relax and take him even deeper, my tongue swiping over his tight balls and making him groan. Shoving his thighs apart, I slide my tongue lower. Tracing it around his puckered hole as spit drips from my lips and down his crease.

Slowly, I work a finger inside of his tight hole. To my absolute delight, I earn another longer moan, and my dick becomes impossibly hard.

Easing another finger into his ass to stretch him, Hail practically writhes for me. "I want to bury my dick here," I rasp.

His head lifts, eyes wide. He gives me a frantic nod. "Take it. Fuck me, Z. I'm yours."

Hot blood rushes through me, my dick throbbing in my constraining boxers. I slide them off and toss them onto the concrete, giving him a full view of just how much he is wrecking me.

Climbing back onto his perfect body, I lower my palm to his mouth. "Make it wet for me."

His eyes flash with lust as his tongue slicks me over. I run it along my length. Driven by wild emotion, I spit down his balls and into his crease. Then I press the swollen crown of my cock to his puckered hole.

Slowly, shaking with barely restrained control, I push in. Just a little. I give him a few breaths between incremental movements of my hips. I'm already close to detonating just from the idea of being inside of him, but I squeeze my eyes shut and focus on not exploding.

"So fucking tight, Hails."

"No teasing," he pleads. Gripping my ass in both hands, he pulls himself onto my dick with a wince.

Fuckkk me. Pleasure builds low in my spine. I shudder, fighting to keep from unloading my balls into his ass prematurely. My hips draw back, the tight constriction of him around me absolute heaven, and then I drive back in.

I never expected to feel this way about anyone. This is everything. *He* is everything. And I don't want to lose him again.

Hail rocks his hips to meet my thrusts as I find a rhythm. He's letting out these little noises that fucking ruin me internally. How could I run from this? He would never hurt me intentionally. He only wanted to help me. My fucking fault for not setting hard limits for myself, though maybe I needed to cross a few lines...

There's quite a few still in my way.

He loops an arm around my neck, crushing my mouth to his. His tongue slides against my own, wiping my brain of thoughts until we're nothing more than movement and raw emotion and delicious pleasure.

I reach a hand down to grip his cock and stroke it as I piston into him. I want him to feel just as much as I do while I'm buried in his tight heat. He lets out a growl, much like the one he unleashes on stage. Only this one is for me alone.

I drop my forehead to his collarbone. "I'm too close."

"We have all the time in the world to keep doing this," he pants, his fearful amber eyes finding mine. I put that there. Made him so afraid. "Please tell me we do."

"We do," I say, placing a lingering kiss on his neck, but I only half believe the words coming out of my mouth.

I have to get better. I have to deal with my shit or I will never stop disappointing Hail. Which means I would be disappointing Liam, and all of Atonement, too.

I can't keep touring with them. It's been a trigger for me, one that I obviously can't navigate on my own.

Putting my all into the last few thrusts, I moan as my own release shatters me. Hail follows me over the edge as I peg his prostate.

Gasping for breath, he drops his hands out wide on the dock, completely spent. "I didn't know it could feel like that."

I slip out of him and help him wriggle back into his soaked boxers. I do the same until we're somewhat dressed and shivering again. Hand firmly clasped in his, I lead him up to the bed-and-breakfast.

The owner looks both of us up and down as we walk in her front door, sated and dripping ocean water on her wooden floors. Her eyes go wide a bit at the sight of Hail, tattooed and pierced and looking like fucking sex personified in just his boxers.

"How do I get one of those?" she asks, motioning to all of him. "Did you fish him out of the Atlantic?"

We both smirk, and then she waves us down the hall to the bedrooms. "Lunch will be out in a bit, boys. Go get dried off."

We take our time in the hot shower, jacking each other off because the chemical attraction between us is inescapable.

Afterwards, we dress in joggers and band shirts, both rocking Atonement's abstract logo. Perched on the edge of the bed, Hail cocks his head at me. "I like that look on you a little too much." He smiles, hands roving down to squeeze my ass and drag me into a tender kiss. Then he gently kisses my split brow and bruised chin.

Pulling away, my stomach winds into knots. "What are you doing here, Hails?"

His brows furrow. "Retrieving you."

"You're in the middle of a tour."

He shrugs. "I don't give a shit."

I press the heels of my palms against my closed eyes and give a heavy sigh. "You have to go back."

His head shakes frantically, wet locks swaying. I can't help but push them out of his face. "Not without you, sunshine. Malek can handle leading for a while. The fans shouldn't be too pissed. Hell, it's a good test to see if me taking more of a backseat would plummet sales." His features scrunch up in the cutest way.

Closing the distance between us, I draw him into another kiss. "I have to straighten myself out. This isn't... this isn't healthy. For either of us."

Muscles twitch along his jaw, but I soothe them with light strokes of my fingers.

"Please, Hail. I need you to understand. I don't want to keep hurting you. But right now, you're the only reason I want to live." I lick my lips and shake my head. "And I know... I know that's not okay."

After a span of silence, he finally nods. "Okay."

Hail

After we're treated to a savory lunch of stew and vegetables, courtesy of the bed-and-breakfast owner, I buy a plane ticket and fire off a message to Liam. Then Z and I catch a bus back to Dublin. His head rests on my shoulder as we snuggle down in the seat and watch the ancient stone buildings and random castles drift by.

Roaming Dublin's streets, we actually get lost. My phone isn't getting any service and Z doesn't offer to pull up a map on his phone. I would complain, but what if his service got shut off or something? I don't want to make him feel bad.

Anyway, it's probably for the best that he's cut off from everyone right now. The media's gone too far with his story, addicted to the mysterious disappearance and downfall of Zander Graves, and I'm not sure how to put a stop to it short of causing some cataclysmic disaster.

Maybe I *should* get arrested. Somehow, I still think the media will blame him for it.

I check my phone again, my text to Liam left unsent. "Ugh, it irks me when people's cell phones stop working in horror movies. Like no way that's realistic. But here we are. No service. Liam's going to send a swat team after me."

Rain smacks against my forehead, and I can't help but crack a smile at Z, quiet and brooding at my side.

"Just great. Fucking weather," he mumbles, shaking damp hair from his eyes. His little dangly earring swings, and my heart skips a beat. If only he understood just how much I love seeing a piece of me on him. "What?"

"We're in Dublin. No show tonight. No flight until tomorrow."

"We're rained out of the touristy things I wanted to share with you before you fly out."

I turn toward him. "Oh my god, are you pouting?"

"No." His lip juts out. "Yes."

I catch his jaw in my hand and lean in to bite his soft, full bottom lip. "I have you to myself. That's all I ever need."

Taking his hand, I tug him into the first hotel I can find–a quaint, four-story stone building.

"What are we doing?" Z demands, glancing around the Victorian interior, crackling with a warm fire. A handful of families enjoy tea at fine dining tables on one end of the main floor, and two heavy oak desks with waiting employees are positioned on either side of the massive fireplace.

"Living in the moment," I whisper, giving his hand a reassuring squeeze.

Swallowing, he fumbles after me into the small, creaking elevator once I purchase a room. When the doors part to our floor, I take his hand again and kiss the back of it.

"I know you're secretly happy about this, so stop with the frown," I say, shutting our bedroom door to trap us in the small, outdated room with plush carpet and a four poster bed.

His smile is solemn. "I'm just... going to miss this."

My heart plummets. "Don't you dare talk like this is goodbye."

Z goes quiet, and I fight the urge to storm over to him and demand that he promise me this isn't our end.

Instead, I swallow down those sickening emotions and connect to Wi-Fi so we can order food. We devour two pizzas and sprawl out on the bed, naturally falling into work on a few songs. Z's fighting to find fault with his lyrics, sliding the pen over the cupid's bow of his lips in the most distracting way.

I play with his hair while he reads his lyrics out loud.

You are a black hole

Within you, I can see my demise

And still, I'm enraptured

Drowning in those whiskey eyes

Unable to escape my fate

All I can do is cling to you and ready my heart

Because one day I know I'll let you tear me apart

"That's not about me, is it?" I ask, pinching at his side. "Cause the only thing I want to tear into is that ass."

Z snorts and rolls his eyes. "You're so romantic."

"Have I told you today how perfect you are?" Grinning, I flip him onto his back, straddling his hips and pinning his arms above his head. "I want to show you just how perfect we can be together."

I kiss him slowly, not wanting to rush this. He's mine for the entire night. This is what I've come to crave. Easy nights with him. Hotel rooms and takeout. Bad movies and sweet, stolen moments in between, even though we both knew there was a deadline to us.

But what if there wasn't? What if Z would agree to this life with me? Continue writing songs and traveling with me once he gets better? It's a dream I want more than anything. My missing puzzle piece.

My hands roam down his smooth body, savoring the feel of him and aching to root myself in the present. He's breathing hard already as his gaze watches me touch all of my favorite places on his body. I dip low to let my tongue swirl over his nipple, then give it a bite. I work the other one over as he lets his head fall back in defeat, his dick hard beneath me.

"Let me take care of you," I murmur onto his skin.

I trail heated kisses along his collarbone and up his neck. I grip his jaw and then move my lips until they're hovering over the corner of his mouth.

A smile takes hold of me as he trembles in anticipation.

"I live for that reaction, Z." Reaching for his hand, I direct it over my heart. He tilts his head slightly to meet my gaze, his eyes widening over how fast my own heart's beating for him. "See how you bring me to life?"

His Adam's apple bobs, and then I lock my lips to his. Working him open, I suck at the tip of his tongue. One of my hands drifts lower to grip his cock between us. My body soon follows. I lick my way up and down his shaft. Then I toy with sucking his crown into my mouth, just enough to get him antsy before I drive my mouth down as far as I can take him.

He quivers and moans. It doesn't take long before he's pumping warm cum down my throat. I swallow it greedily. *Mine. All mine.*

I move back up to claim his mouth, wanting him to taste himself on my lips. My hands push his bent legs further up so he's fully exposed for me. I tease him, sliding my hard dick along his ass.

"I need you inside of me," he whimpers against my forceful mouth.

"Say it again. Beg for me."

"Hails. *Please.* Please fuck me."

I hum in approval, then lean back to grab the bottle of lube we purchased during our wandering. And *no*, I didn't giggle like a schoolgirl when I paid for it. Hell, Z wouldn't even walk up to the counter with me.

Squirting some into my hand, I run drenched fingers between his cheeks, circling his hole a few times before easing a finger in. I pump it slowly a few times, Z already moving beneath me. When he's properly stretched, I line up and start to push into him. Gripping his hips, I tilt his ass up slightly and begin rolling into him, setting an easy pace.

"Hails." He pants my name as his hands settle on my knees. His fingers hook behind them to pull himself further onto my cock. But I keep our rhythm punishingly slow.

"All night, Z," I tell him. "You have me all night."

Despite my plan, I'm unable to keep from shooting my load into his ass after a couple more minutes of decadent thrusts. We collapse in a heap, laid out on the bed.

"I can't imagine a life without you, sunshine," I admit. "I'm sorry if those words cause you trouble."

I prop my body up on my forearms in time to catch tears glistening in his eyes. I cradle his face in my hand. "You've got me, Z. My heart and soul belong to you."

A tear slips down his cheek like a falling star. I catch it on the tip of my finger. "Don't give me something so precious," he whispers.

"Go ahead and wreck me then, because I'm not going anywhere."

He embraces me, pulling me tight against him. Holding me for countless breaths and beats of our hearts. "I don't want to keep hurting you. Hails, I need to get better."

I want to rage against this truth. To tell him I can fix him. I can carry all of his pain.

I cling to him tighter. "I know. Just let me hold you a little while longer before I set you free."

After two more orgasms, I end up sprawled over Hail's lap. The way he's staring down at me and twirling locks of my hair around his fingers has me itching to spill my own truths. Would I feel lighter if I shared them?

"You asked about my family in the beginning," I say hesitantly, dread slithering through my chest. "My dad left when I was twelve. My mum says it's because I was gay. He considered taking my brother with him, but when Lex stood his ground—supported me—he chose to leave us all behind."

I suck in a breath as Hail looks down at me, half in shock. I push through the discomfort, gripping the bedsheets in both hands.

"Lex drowned in a pool after someone gave him weed laced with fentanyl at a party. Mum went after the guy that owned the property. When she didn't get any money, she turned her hatred fully on me. Rightfully so, I cost her a husband and the better son."

Hail's hand balls into a fist on my chest. "She blamed you."

"I *am* responsible. I was five years older. He was only seventeen. He was allowed in the band because I promised Mum I would watch over him. And when he was gone, my mum couldn't deal. She attempted suicide. Between that and, well, the drinking prior to that, I sent her to a place to get better. I wanted to help, but even after she came home, she wasn't the same."

"Jesus," Hail utters. "Have you talked to anyone about this?"

I roll my head back and forth over his muscled thigh, right over the spot where I left a hickey earlier.

His brows knead together. "Not even your bandmates?"

"I couldn't stand the idea of them hating me more. I was a dick to all of them. I was horrible to Lex right before... I left him out by the pool alone, knowing he wasn't right in the head. Knowing he needed help. I tore my family apart. It wasn't right of me to seek any sort of relief from that pain."

Closing my eyes, I see his body calmly floating beneath the surface like a dream. No one told you that death could be so fucking peaceful sometimes. It's the thought of what came before his last breath that will forever disturb me. My fucked up brain wants to know–did he fight? Did he know those were his final moments as he sank to the bottom? Or was he too messed up to realise he was dying?

"I fled. Wandered all over Europe all the way up until two months ago. Thought I could lie low for the rest of my pathetic existence." I draw in a sharp breath. "My selfishness cost the band their futures, too."

Hails shakes his head. "That's fucked up and you know it. You know that, right?"

A hoarse laugh escapes me. "I don't know that," I say honestly, rubbing at my tired eyes.

"Did no one try to reach out to you? They couldn't have just let you vanish."

"They tried. I didn't respond. How could they forgive me? You saw our bassist. The guy that decked me in the hotel lobby? And even if they did somehow understand, being around them would just be another dagger to my bleeding heart. Another reminder that there's a hole where Lex used to exist. I wouldn't be able to ignore his absence anymore. Those little pauses, those moments of silence between all of us, they would fucking ruin me, Hails. Not to mention, I had been struggling with an addiction to drugs and alcohol for a while."

My chin wobbles and a muscle in Hail's jaw twitches. "So you've been clinging to denial and keeping yourself isolated?"

I nod, meeting his eyes. They're filled with tears, too. Suddenly, I'm struck with the need to move. To feel more pain. To numb everything inside of me just to rid myself of this fucking gnarled mess of emotions I can't untangle. It makes me want to claw my skin off. Cut through it with something sharp. Heal something within me just so I can break it again.

Gone. Lex is gone. The one shield I had against the cruel words of my parents for something I didn't *choose.* I shouldn't have used him that way, but Lex was always stronger than me.

Hail drapes his arm over my bare stomach and rests his head against my forearm while I sob. God, how many more times can I cry? How much of me is left to crumble? Isn't there a timestamp on grief? When can I start trusting my brain to feel normal again?

Because this thing with Hail and the support I've received from Atonement? It has only served to lift me up higher so when I fell, cause I always do, the more my bones shattered.

I know that's fucked up thinking, blaming them for showing me a sliver of happiness. I know pushing them away isn't the answer. But dragging Hail down with me every time I plummet into this abyss isn't good for his health, either.

"I've tried so hard in all the wrong ways, all the *easy* ways, to fix my stupid fucking brain." I smash a fist against my temple.

He catches my wrist when I go to hit myself again. "Jesus. Please stop doing that."

I shudder against him. "I know what I *need* to do. It's the courage I'm lacking."

Running the hem of his shirt between my fingers, I keep thinking about the business card Liam gave me that's still tucked in my wallet. I should make that phone call sooner rather than later because I know I'll find a way to talk myself out of seeking help.

Sometime during our cuddling, we shimmy under the blankets, completely drained both mentally and physically. I blink into the darkness. As if sensing my troubled thoughts, Hail tucks me closer against his body.

"Hey, sunshine," he says, kissing my temple.

"Hey, Hails."

His thumb caresses my bare hip bone. "I love you."

Those three words, so easily given to me. I stretch up to kiss his cheek.

"Thank you, but I think I might love you more," I whisper back.

He sighs, and I feel his chest rise and fall with a shaky breath. "Selfishly, I hope you come back to me soon, but however long it takes, I'll always be waiting for you."

Thirty-Three

Hail

ONE MONTH LATER

Only when we have breaks in our tour do I realize how much I rely on others to entertain me.

We get five whole days off for Thanksgiving. It's the longest break we've had since I can last remember, and I've already decided that I'm going to spend 4.75 of those days nagging Liam to hang out, which I know is going to require more gym time than I prefer. I'm pretty sure the guy holds permanent residence there.

Get ready to see me jacked, Z.

For some unknown reason, maybe because I'm a masochist, I agreed to my sister's request to attend one family dinner. While I'm always hesitant to visit home, I'll never turn down the chance to spend time with my twin.

There's also a little itch in my brain that wants me to tell my family about Z. How much I want to keep him.

I sprint across my parents' manicured lawn to scoop Stasi up in a bear hug. Lifting her, I spin her around and let out a menacing growl that definitely makes the neighbors debate calling the police. Sun hats and visors pop up all around us behind sprinklers and tornados of grass trimmings, their laser eyes focused on the "riff raff" that just got out of a black muscle car with too much tint.

Liam leans against the driver's side, sunglasses on, and folds his tattooed arms over his massive chest.

"You're thirty minutes late," Stasi complains when I finally set her down. Her attention drifts to Liam. She lifts a hand and gives a shy smile. "Hey."

"Stasi," he replies.

Her cheeks flush with rosy color, and my head whips between them. Surely I've mistaken Liam's sultry tone.

"Oh, hell no!" I jab a finger in his direction. "Take the fucking sunglasses off!"

"I'd rather not."

"You'd better not be checking out my sister, then. I'll put you in a choke-hold."

Cool as a fucking cucumber, Liam pushes off his car and opens the driver's door. "No offense, Hail, but out of the three of us, you'd be the last to win in a fight. And Stasi's a grown woman. She can imagine me naked all she wants."

I'm pouting as he gets in his car and speeds off, turning heads. I can practically taste the HOA's fury brewing.

I mean, Stasi is *ripped*. Lean, but definitely a fucking threat.

"You, uh, get a job as security at an MMA dojo or something?" I ask, scratching at my chin.

Stasi's laugh is light, and it makes my heart soar. "No, but I do spend my free time between classes working off stress. Now get your ass inside."

Stepping up to the door, I suck in a deep breath, planning to hold it through the entirety of this meal. It's been a long time since I've visited home.

Stasi gives my hand a squeeze. "Hail. This has nothing to do with you, but Max canceled last minute. And as far as Dad goes, just don't let him get to you, okay?"

"Easier said than done," I mutter. I know for a fact Max backed out because he found out I was coming. To this day, my family won't accept that I'm not in some sort of cult—biting heads off bats and snorting lines out of hookers' ass cracks.

And if Max isn't going to be here, that means the focus will be all on me.

My aunt and uncle are already seated with my mom and dad at the formal table in the dining room, which smells faintly like expensive Cuban cigars. They all look me over when I stride in, fingers trailing the wainscoting, so I take them in as well to prove I'm not intimidated. My uncle is dressed down for once in a Packers shirt—I'm sure that pisses Stasi off—and my aunt has a silly floppy sun hat on, which I can tell is pissing my mom off across the table. My mom keeps fiddling with the rings around the cloth napkins she set out.

"Mykhail!" my mother forces out, coming over to give me an awkward hug. Stasi and I got our light hair and rich eyes from her. "We were just talking about you."

My father grunts and digs his knife into his steak. His blonde hair is more silvery-white now, and he's lost significant weight. "More tattoos, I see. Is any of that necessary?"

Breaking out the mask I used to wear when I lived under *his* roof, I shrug and crack a toothy grin. "Makes me feel cool."

Stasi flashes me a grin and we sit down–me furthest from my father, who refuses to acknowledge the contributions I make to small talk. My aunt asks about the tour, and I gladly fill her in on the places we've visited. My mom oooh's and ahhh's and throws in little comments like I've told her any of this information, but she only gets clips of my life through Stasi and the messages I've sent her that go unanswered.

I can't help but think about Z and how his mother has treated him, and it steels me against anything my parents could ever do to me. Sometimes the ones that should love us most are the ones that cut us the deepest. But there's no written rule that says you have to keep letting them dig that knife in.

I miss Z. He made me promise not to call or text him for a while. He wanted space to focus on sorting out his trauma with Liam's therapist.

I can't help but wonder how things are going. If he's making any progress. If the media's still hung up on pestering him when he's trying his best to heal for good this time.

An idea strikes me. If they're going to hang on the topic, we might as well shift the focus from his past onto the present and give them something positive to talk about.

I pull out my phone under the dining table and leak through social media that I'll be doing raw online performances of songs Zander Graves and I wrote this evening. I give them the truths about our relationship. The unfathomable depth of my love for that guy. I ask them to respectfully share their reactions and love for him as he battles mental illness.

It's the most raw and transparent I've been with our fans, and I pray my message is well-received. I hope they can find it in their hearts to shower Z with the support he deserves.

"Lizbeth just moved back to town," my father comments loudly, breaking my focus from my phone. "Broke it off with that last boyfriend she had. Her father said she got a job here as a marketing director."

I fight against a sour expression at the casual way he's brought up my ex. I know the direction we're headed. If I haven't disappointed him with my lack of education and career choice, then I've let him down by not marrying his colleague's daughter. You know, the one that cheated on me with her boss.

Not like my father's colleague would even allow me within ten feet of his daughter with all the ink on my body now.

"Oh, she's such a lovely girl! Single, too," my mother adds. "Maybe she could help clear up all that recent bad press surrounding you."

"Arrived at this topic in record time," I mutter, reaching for my drink to fix the dryness in my throat. Stasi shifts in her seat and drops her gaze to her food.

"She's a good match for you, Mykhail. It's time you consider what your future looks like," my dad continues.

No need to bring up the fact that I make enough income to retire in my thirties. That's the thing, my parents don't know that. They don't know anything about me or my journey with music. It is so far outside of their scope, and they're not comfortable even meeting me halfway if it means leaving their invisible, perfect little box.

"My future is in music, Artem," I reply firmly, throwing out my father's name like I'm actually in charge.

"Eventually, that will dry up, and you'll be some washed up loser on the side of the street begging for money and probably strung out on drugs," my dad snaps back. His sharp gray eyes cut to me. "You're not on drugs already, are you?"

I tilt my head back and let out a tired laugh. "Alright, you know what? I'm fucking done."

"Mykhail! Language!" my mother scolds.

I scoot my chair back and lean down to give Stasi a kiss on the cheek. "I'll call you later, yeah?"

She nods, tight-lipped. "Sorry, Hail."

"It's not your fault." I let my gaze sweep over the table. "Just so you stop pushing the matter. I'm bi-sexual. I'm in love with a guy. And get ready for it cause this is really the cherry on top. He's in the music industry, too. Go ahead and pass that message along to Max so he can join in the crucifixion."

Silverware drops onto my father's plate. "For fuck's sake."

I don't even let him get in another dig. Striding out the front door, I don't look back. There's a tug of concern for my sister, but she actively chooses to still partake in this family. Though it feels like betrayal, I'm not going to force her to pick sides.

Liam's already waiting for me, his Pantera pulled up against the curb like he never left. He rolls his window down.

"Record time, huh?" His smile belongs to the devil.

I can't fight back my own impish grin as I hop in his car. He hands me his pair of Armani sunglasses and retrieves another pair from a new case.

"What is this about?" I ask, the sunglasses pinched between my frozen fingers as I peek over at him.

He keeps his gaze forward as he shifts into gear. "Bought another pair. Keep them this time."

I crack a grin and slide them on, feeling like a million bucks as Liam burns out, leaving skid marks on the street in front of my parent's driveway.

"Oh, I probably should have asked first, but I kind of announced releasing a couple of songs tonight." I brace for the lecture, but Liam only nods. "Figured we could use some of your recording equipment."

"I already saw. I think you should take a look at your post."

Brows furrowed, I open up social media.

"Holy shit." My heart swells in my chest at the love already pouring out of our fans. Not just Atonement's fans, but hardcore loyal fans of Visage, too. Everyone's sharing songs from their old album and begging for Zander's return.

When I lift my head back up, my eyes shoot wide open as I take in the empty parking lot Liam pulls into. There's a crazy cool mural painted on the brick wall facing the street, a collage of music notes and records and brutal looking angels levitating on razor-sharp wings. There are pieces of Atonement and Visage woven into the images, and I already sense the oncoming wave of tears.

"What is this?" I ask quietly, sniffling.

Liam removes his sunglasses, and I catch the mischievous reddish glint in his dark brown eyes. "My new studio. Let's go record your hits."

My heart has turned to goo, but I still slam his car door shut to hammer home my point. "You're kidding me. You really fucking hid the fact that you bought a fancy ass recording studio? Do Malek and Griff know?"

He shrugs. "They'll find out tonight. Already sent them the address. Pizza's on the way, too."

I shake my head, cursing under my breath as he pulls out his keys and unlocks the front door. In a way, he's a lot like Z. He keeps himself tucked away. Keeps his demons buried deep, some of them still unknown to me, despite the fact that I've been friends with the guy forever.

But witnessing Liam's growth over the years, seeing where he's at now, gives me hope that Z will get here, too.

When the clock hits midnight and we launch two heart-wrenching singles with clean vocals into the world, hot tears prick my eyes at the overwhelming positivity everyone is sending Z's way. I hope it will give him the strength to come back to me soon.

And I hope everyone out there suffering from invisible wounds like Z and Liam, can find the self-love they deserve.

Thirty-Four

Love Letters

Hey there, sunshine!

I'm ashamed at how long it took me to find a loophole in this whole no texts or calls agreement.

If you thought I was going to forget you just because you're across a mother-fucking ocean, you're so wrong. And because it took my dumbass over a month to figure out how to communicate with you without breaking my promise, get ready for a whole boatload of letters, Z! Not just from me, but from supporting fans, too. There's literally nothing you can do about it (maniacal laughter).

I mean, you could shred the letters, but I feel like you're more of a stuff them in a shoebox and hide them in a closet type of guy. You fancy words too much to destroy them.

Also, sorry for using Liam's PI to track you down again. I wanted to know that you were safe. I had a bit of a meltdown a week into leaving you. Honestly, I'm still fighting the urge to jump on a plane and come to where you are.

I'll be good, I promise. As long as you need me to be. And when you're back in my arms, maybe we'll read all of my crap letters and laugh at my disgustingly sweet devotion to you. Liam thinks I'm pathetic.

Other than the fact that I miss you, things are okay here. Liam and I recorded two of the songs you wrote and did a "soft release" on them. They are being so well-received!

I had a heart-to-heart with Malek and Griff about my desire to take a backseat for a while. Would you believe I'm now Atonement's lead guitarist? Probably not long-term. Especially not if you want the job. I'll happily step aside and cheer my fucking heart out for you.

We actually had an overwhelming amount of people audition for vocals, and I cannot wait for you to meet our pick. Maria is an absolute beast! If you haven't heard her yet, can you wait to listen to her with me? I want to see your reaction. Though, Malek and Griff really need to lay off the flirting and realize they're in a business relationship with her.

Oh wait, HA!

Anyway, the weather has cooled down here, finally, and it just makes me ache for you even more. I miss our cozy movie nights and music wormholes and coffee shop visits and park adventures. I sound so old, don't I? Why don't we just book a permanent table at the Cracker Barrel already? You probably don't know what that is, but that's okay. We'll hit that place up soon.

I love you. Please keep fighting.

- Hails

Hails,

You would find a way to circumvent rules. But I'm glad you did. I've proven I don't make good decisions, and my choice to try to keep all communication from you was wrong. So I'm sorry for that. You're always fighting for me, and I'm always running away.

Honestly, your letter came when I was lurking in another low. My therapist warned things might get worse before they get better. We're delving into topics I've kept buried for too long, and it hurts. It hurts to talk about it, Hails.

But I've been speaking with her as much as she'll see me, and I joined an AA group here. I can honestly say my periods of feeling bad have gotten less frequent. I don't feel like I'm drowning in guilt at all hours of the day. I don't feel the urge to numb my emotions, either. It's amazing how ignorant I had become to the negativity I allowed to fester in my brain. We're slowly working on that, too.

But until I can face my mum and cut off financial ties, I don't think I'm able to move forward. While I'm counting down the days until I can come home to you, I know I have to work through my problems fully. I don't want to hurt you the way I did when I left you. I want to be rock solid for you.

Selma says hi. She's in love with our songs. We listened to them together at her place. Somehow, I've agreed to Friday movie nights with her.

I promise I'll wait to look up anything new by Atonement.

In other news, I picked up part-time work at a music studio teaching lessons. Go ahead and be jealous of me for stealing one of your dreams. It makes me feel like a part of you was here with me. Besides therapy, it's become my reason for getting out of bed in the morning. No, I'm still not an early bird. Yes, I'm working on it.

However, teaching music to kids in between writing songs has been surprisingly uplifting. The things they say, Hails. I swear I've never laughed so hard in my life. They don't care that I was almost famous and now I'm washed up. They only care that I make a fool of myself by pretending to mess up notes. One kid snorted so hard he farted and cleared out the entire room. Another one reminds me a lot of myself, and I hope I'm making a difference in his life.

Anyway, the weather is cool here too. I miss snuggling with you.

If Cracker Barrel is on the same level as Snooze, save me a permanent seat.

You'll always have my heart, though I hope one day soon I can give you all of it.

Love,

Your Sunshine (yes, that made me cringe to write. Are you happy?)

Sunshine,

I am so happy. You have no idea. I literally cannot stop smiling after reading your letter. Thank you for writing me back. I had braced for silence, telling myself the knowledge that you were alive and had an address would be enough.

And teaching music lessons, Z? That is incredible! You are a gift to those children, I'm certain of it.

We finished our U.S. tour. FINALLY. Liam and I have been booking some local musicians at the studio while Atonement works on our next album. It feels good to keep it low key. Maybe I am management material after all, Dad!

There's this house down the street in a new construction neighborhood. It's small, but it has a built-in grill and a pool! I think I might inquire about it, but only if you think it's a good idea. I don't want to make big decisions without your input. You are a part of my life.

Oh! And Max actually let me see my niece! Well, it was really Stasi. They asked her to babysit while they were off at some work conference, and Stasi let me come over. I'm not sure that was wise, because now I'm wrapped around that kid's tiny finger, and I'm not sure I'll get to see her again.

But Stasi's been talking to Max about how I'm moving into a management role, and while it's not right, I think Max may come around to me soon. I'm the proper kind of human now!

Anyway, I won't lie and say this long distance thing has been easy. Not that I would ever give up on you. Just saying how I feel. I want to hold you. Kiss you. Touch you. Love you in person.

- Hails

Hails.

You didn't warn me.

Pretty certain the postman is plotting to assassinate me. Over two-hundred letters? Took me two weeks to read them all. I don't think I've ever cried that hard. I do a lot of that, don't I?

Happy to hear you're enjoying the slower pace. You deserve the rest, metal god.

Text me pics of the house. I'd love to see it. Maybe we should switch over to text or FaceTime. Give the postman a break for a bit. You can tell me all about meeting your niece, and we can dissect what a dickhead your brother is.

Things are good. I feel good, though I miss you more than I could have imagined.

Love,

Zander

THIRTY–FIVE

SEVEN MONTHS LATER

I'm standing outside my childhood home.

Regardless of the outcome today, I know it's necessary for me to exchange some words with my mother, so I can shed the chains she's wrapped around me using Lex's death as an excuse to allow her to wallow in the past.

Stepping up to the doorbell, I let my eyes peruse the red brick exterior, the patterned glass window to my second story window, and the uniform bushes that match the rest of the identical houses on the narrow street.

Mum opens the door and her scowl turns down even more.

"You've got a lot of fucking nerve. What do you want?" Her voice is harsher than I remember. Guess that will happen to you when you smoke a pack a day for two decades.

"Can we talk?" I push the words out in an even tone, shoving down my pain until she will properly hear it.

She hesitates, eyes surveying the quiet, manicured neighbourhood like she can't stand the idea of being seen with me. Eventually, she lets me inside. I try not to hover in the stuffy hallway where pictures of a young Lex dangle from the wall. When we reach the small kitchen, she sits down at the table. I stifle a cough as she lights up a cigarette immediately.

"How have you been?" I ask, taking in the new wrinkles on her face. The frizzy black hair curling out from her messy bun. I haven't seen her since dropping her off at J. Flowers Health Institute years ago. The bags under her eyes are more prominent, and there are packs of cigarettes stacked on the kitchen counter, along with ashtrays, all over the stuffy, dust-coated living room.

She puffs out a thick cloud of smoke. "Could be better. Dishwasher went out last month."

There's a request in that comment, one she lets linger. Was she always this cold and callous? Was there ever a time that she loved me? Or was my coming out the excuse she needed to stop pretending to care for me, the child she never wanted?

I was the needy one, after all. The one with colic. The one that cried all the way up until age seven, clinging to her skirts when she would drop me off at school or aftercare. The one that had recurring nightmares and kept her from sleeping. The one that refused to finish the meal she prepared because textures bothered me.

The one that admitted to liking a guy at school.

Could she at least pretend to want me here? I mean, I get that she's only after the money, but could she make that less obvious?

Though, it's somewhat of a relief knowing I can finally close this chapter on my life for good. I have the power to stop letting her manipulate me.

"I can't keep supporting you," I finally say, hating the taste of the words on my tongue.

She blinks at me through a cloud of smoke. "What."

"Once I'm done paying off J. Flowers, I'm not sending you any more money. I'm not going to enable you to sit around in your own pain and do nothing."

Her hands begin to tremble. "You're fucking kidding me, right?"

"Mum, you need to find a job—"

"Get the fuck out of my house."

I sigh, sadness and hurt rising up inside me. After a few moments of practiced breaths, I let the emotions pass. Then I meet her heated gaze.

"I'm sorry. For everything. For not being the child you wanted. For my failure with Lex—"

"Get the fuck out!" Her hand tremors as she points toward the front door.

Summoning the strength I've been building in preparation for this day, I forge on. "I don't think I'll ever shed the guilt for that night. But I hope one day you can understand that I would never, ever do anything intentionally to harm you or him. I hope one day you can forgive me."

She rises from her chair, all fire and brimstone. "Out, now! And don't you fucking come back here again! You worthless, murderous child—"

Calmly, I move for the front door. I close it behind me and inhale a deep breath of cool air. I linger on the porch to filter through what I'm feeling, permitting myself the space to analyse my thoughts before they can have a detrimental impact.

Months ago, I would have locked myself in a bathroom and contemplated ways to drown out the pain. Right now? Nothing has a hold of me except a buoyant feeling growing in my chest.

I send a text to my AA sponsor letting the older man know that I'm okay. That's another thing I've learned during my healing process. The importance of communication. Opening up to others has never been easy for me, but I'm learning. I want to learn.

Testing myself further, I head to the cemetery to hunt down Lex's stone. It takes me a while to find it since I wasn't present at his funeral. That would have meant admitting that he was dead.

I lean down and place my hand on his smooth stone. Tears spill from my eyes, but I don't experience the usual crushing desire to stop breathing. To stop living.

"I'm so fucking sorry. I miss you every second of the day, Lex."

With my last ties to London severed, and Selma's blessing to go get my man back, I call a cab to take me to the airport. I've got a surprise opening set for this super famous band called Atonement and endless breakfast dates with a guy I'm madly in love with.

A whispered plea left unanswered

My duty sacrificed for the promise of pleasure

I become the eyes that watch

The hands that shove

The callous will that holds you under

I exist to be your downfall

Yeah, so I can become your saviour

I'm trembling when I finish holding the final note of the last song I wrote with Visage. When my gaze roves over the crowd in the sold-out venue, they're teary-eyed as they shout back at me.

I'm not sure what I feel at first. Maybe hollow? Still a bit haunted, but not to the point where I feel like I need to erase myself. And that gives me hope.

My gaze sweeps to Hail standing at the edge of the stage where Sondra placed him as I took centre stage. My arrival tonight was kept a secret at my request, no matter how hard it was to stay away from him for another fucking minute. Maria keeps popping her head around him from behind, eager to capture his reaction on her phone for social media. She's a whirlwind of personality I haven't quite adjusted to, but I don't think she's going to give me a choice in this friendship.

Tears stream down Hail's face. I tip my head in question, and then he's charging across the stage. Cora takes my guitar in time for me to fully return Hail's embrace. Letting out a sob, he buries his head in my neck. I kiss his cheek a dozen times, desperate to brand myself onto every bit of his skin.

"I missed you," I whisper, clutching him tighter.

He laughs through his heaving, messy crying. "Not as much as I missed you."

He pulls back, and I take his face in both hands and draw him into a kiss in front of thousands of witnesses.

Zander Graves is laid bare for all to see. Nothing left to hide. Nothing left to pick apart. Nothing left to drag me down.

Shrieks of joy erupt from the crowd, and I let out a full laugh, one that has Hail easing back with wide eyes like he's seeing me for the first time. We've chatted over FaceTime almost every day since I reopened that line of communication, but it must be a bit of a shock to see me so carefree in person.

"Want to give them another song?" I ask, brushing a thumb over one of his tears and kissing the damp trail it leaves on his cheek.

We both take the stage as Atonement files out behind us, launching into a song we messed around with on the bus months ago. The crowd is practically frothing at the mouth over the new material, and I fucking love it. I can't help but smile out at them, grateful they've accepted me and all of my faults. All of my darkness. I'm grateful they have it in their hearts to give me a second chance at living.

THREE MONTHS LATER

The doors to the recording studio Liam purchased with cold, hard cash burst open.

Stasi appears with a sack of fast food, coated in a sheen of Texan sweat, and cringes when I shoot daggers at her with my eyes, my fingers pointing to the glowing red recording sign. Liam doesn't even offer her a glance, something he's taken to doing a lot since he's become a full-time resident in Dallas.

My brain is at war on that matter. Check back in another time.

I draw my attention back to Z behind the glass of the recording booth. He's lost in the melody of a new single he plans to release soon. As far as writing songs for other artists, he's churned out absolute hits. He even wrote some heavy lyrics for Atonement because Malek got jealous and wanted a piece of him, too.

Maria, Atonement's new vocalist, has taken to him like a puppy dog, constantly hugging on him. I think Z may have found a new best friend, whether he likes it or not. Although, judging by his appreciation for her homemade tamales, he doesn't mind too much. They seem to both have an interest in fashion, too.

When Z cracks his eyes open, they lock on me. I know at my core that I will never be complete until he is bound to me in every way. My fingers drift to my pocket, where there's a box with an onyx ring inside. It even has a black stone set in the band, something I took a risk on.

Churning nerves drive my knee up and down in rapid movement as I sit and watch him. Liam leans over and smacks his huge hand down on it to keep it still. "Quit. You're making me want to smoke."

I give him a heated look. "Proposing's a big deal, Liam. Not like you'd know."

He snorts at that. "Damn right."

I snatch the cigarette from his hands before he lights up and snap it in half. "Don't start that up. You'll stink up the place."

"S'my studio," he mumbles, another cigarette already in his mouth. He flicks his Zippo open and sucks in heavily. A ripple of worry runs through me over Liam's recent behavior. Maybe settling down isn't what he hoped it would be. Regardless, I plan to nag him endlessly about it tomorrow.

When Z gives a thumbs up, I move into the recording booth. He sets his new twelve string guitar aside, and before he can even get up from the stool, I wrap my arms around his waist and lower my mouth to kiss him.

"We're not still recording, are we?" Z whispers against my lips.

I crack a wide smile and nip at his bottom lip. He's got winged eyeliner on that amps up his gothic look. My dick took notice immediately this morning when I stepped out of the shower in our new home and caught him applying it with care in the bathroom mirror. "Mmm, as much as I'd like to hear audio of us together, I don't want to share you with anyone else."

"No?"

I run a hand through his hair, tugging at locks until I have a full view of his angelic face. "Go on a date with me tonight."

He smirks. "What if I have other plans?"

Anger floods my system. "With who?"

"Just some band members from Atonement. You heard of them?" His full smile wrecks me because I know how hard he had to work for it.

I scowl. "Screw them. You're canceling."

"So possessive."

"Forever will be." I kiss him again, passionately, just to get the point across.

There's a knock on the glass, and we break apart, both of us chuckling at a disgruntled Liam on the other side. "Make out all you want. You're still paying by the hour."

LETTER FROM ABIGAIL

Dear Reader,

I sincerely hope you enjoyed this story! Thank you so much for reading. If you're feeling up to it, Amazon & Goodreads reviews are always welcome and such a help to indie authors!

If you didn't catch on, Z is very much inspired by Tim Henson and Vessel from Sleep Token. Their music has been incredibly influential in my life and Vessel's lyricism has touched so many souls, including mine. While I didn't have a set image in my head for Hail, he does share some characteristics with Will Ramos from Lorna Shore, which is funny because he's a huge fan of Sleep Token!

This story consumed me. I wrote it start-to-finish in four weeks, which is insanity for me. But... I'm going to take a page out of Hail's book and be the most raw form of myself here. I think the ease of writing this story came because these boys are each a half of me. Hail is the mask I show the world, goofy and loyal but also in desperate need of approval. Z is what I hide beneath. Though I've never experienced trauma on the level he did, the depth of his depression is something I've fought with since I was a teenager. It's something I still fight with daily. There are thoughts and experiences in Z's story that are true to me. Things I haven't shared with anyone. Fear of my own addictive personality.

Sometimes the shame of what we're feeling can be crippling, too. In a way, writing this story let me come to terms with some of my own demons. And while I haven't found peace with my destructive brain yet, this story allowed me to take some steps necessary to maybe get there one day.

On a lighter note, there are other truths to this story. Real places my husband and I have visited. We had a date on the London Eye and ate fish and chips from a little food truck at the bridge. The cove Z winds up at is based on Dunquin Pier in Ireland. I wouldn't fancy ever taking a dip in that water, but then again, the ocean is terrifying! My husband and I also stayed at the bed & breakfast in Sligo I wrote about. The owner cooked us one of the best breakfasts! Oh, and Hail mentions Iceland's pancakes? Yeah, that's a real thing. Pretty sure we dropped $60 there every morning. I blame pregnancy. And the golf chapter? Inspired by true events with some wild friends we used to terrorize golf courses with, although there was a lot more drinking and chaos involved.

Anyway, Liam and Stasi have their own demons to slay in book two, Raise Me Up, so stay tuned!

You can find my social media links & newsletter sign-up here: https://linktr.ee/abigailglenn

Also by Abigail Glenn

FORGED IN CHAOS, a dual POV dark fantasy romance.

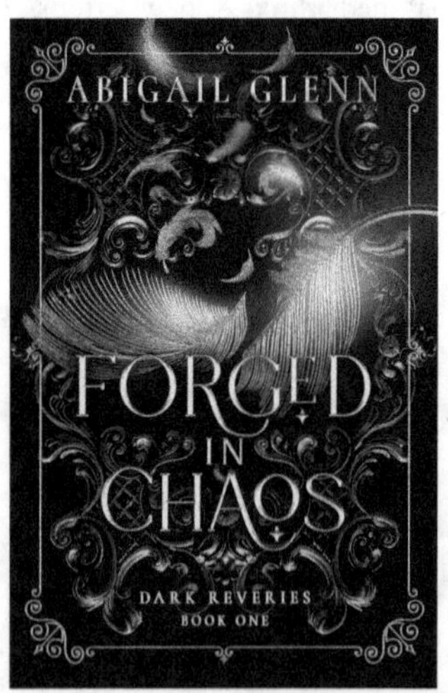

Find my book links & newsletter sign up here:
https://linktr.ee/abigailglenn